COLLECTION OF SHORT STORIES

by

Carol Lodzinski

DORRANCE
PUBLISHING CO
EST. 1920
PITTSBURGH, PENNSYLVANIA 15238

Dorrance Publishing Co
585 Alpha Drive
Suite 103
Pittsburgh, PA 15238
Visit our website at *www.dorrancebookstore.com*

ISBN: 978-1-6853-7168-5
eISBN: 978-1-6853-7711-3

COLLECTION OF SHORT STORIES

by

Carol Lodzinski

CONTENTS

1
CAT AND MOUSE GAMES

Detective Grace Sheffield was new to the precinct and at her best when assigned to a case. But she wasn't working on any case now—she was on a mission.

Special Detective, Joe Rhymes hadn't been pleased being stuck with a rookie, but as time went by, his opinion changed.

"Joe, can I use your computer?" she asked.

"Sure, I was just going to get us some coffee anyway."

Her fingers rapidly went over the keyboard. She was looking for info on an ex-con: Conners, William (Willy), who had lured a five-year-old girl, Jennifer Clayton, from the school grounds, taken her to an abandoned building, beaten, burned, and raped her. It was never disclosed if she was dead before or after being violated, more for her parent's sanity than anything else. He was released from prison three years later due to a technicality, but Detective Sheffield wasn't going to let him off that easy.

"Here's your coffee. What're you working on?" Joe asked, placing the coffee on the desk and looking at the computer screen. "Are you still after that guy? Don't you have better things to do on a Saturday night?"

"How can anyone have a good time with crazies like Willy running around out there?"

"Listen, Grace, there hasn't been anything new on him for years. He's either dead or hiding someplace far away."

"He can't be far enough away. Anyone who does that to a little girl isn't going to just do it once. Besides, Agent Summers received a call about a missing girl spotted by a deserted house in Daymond County. I'm going to check it out."

A soft breeze blew into the room of the abandoned house. The fire had long been burned out, leaving only ashes and a chill in the air as the clock ticked away the seconds. The cat purred while cleaning herself, seemingly unaware of the field mouse crawling up the trellis and into the opened window looking for food and a place to stay for the night. He scurried across the floor towards the kitchen. He stopped, stood on his haunches, shook his head, and wiggled his nose, sniffing the air, taking in the unpleasant smell. He continued on quickly, not wanting to dirty his skinny, bone-like feet on the dust that had accumulated on the wooden floor. He stopped again. The sound of the clock chiming 3:00 frightened him, but only for a moment. He ran under the kitchen table and started nibbling at some crumbs, long stale but belly-filling nonetheless.

The cat crept silently down the hall and into the kitchen, one paw in front of the other ready to strike. Normally, she would have left the mouse alone, but it had been some time since she had anything to eat. She sprang, landing squarely on the mouse digging her back claws into its stomach and her teeth clamped tightly around his neck. With a quick jerk, the mouse got away, running under the refrigerator leaving a trail of blood behind. She licked the drops of blood from the floor. Sooner or later, he would have to come out. She would be waiting.

Detective Sheffield scanned the missing person's files to see if there were any similar incidents only this time scanning in a 100-mile radius that included Daymond County. There it was: Peggy Lynch, five years old, abducted from the neighborhood school yard. She noted the similarities to the Clayton case.

"Look Joe," she shouted. "Here it is. Read this."

Joe walked over, not particularly interested. She had followed many leads, all resulting in dead ends, but after reading the new missing person's report, even he had to admit there was a connection. It would seem Willy was at it again.

"Grace, I don't want you to get your hopes up. Let's just call Detective Summers and give him a heads up, so we won't have any problem getting a search warrant."

Within the hour, arrangements were made, and they were on their way.

The cat raced to the door when she heard footsteps and hoped, this time, the man would give her some food. Instead, he kicked her, sending her across the room. The mouse took the opportunity to run up the stairs. The man followed, going to a partially opened door and walked into a dimly lit room. The mouse scuttled behind and entered stopping only a moment to lick the wounds on his belly. The man approached a bed where little Peggy was crying.

The mouse didn't care what he was going to do to the girl; he was looking for food. He sniffed around finding a gold object thinking it was cheese but wasn't. He would take it anyway. He took it in his mouth and ran back down the stairs, into the living room, up the curtains, and out the window. The cat, now knowing she was not going to be fed, ran after him. The mouse just made it to the mailbox when the cat pounced on him and swallowed hard as the mouse dropped the gold object.

"I hope this isn't another wild goose chase," Joe said. "The informant said he saw a little girl following a cat and entering an abandoned house on Branch Road. Tell you what, if this amounts to something, I'll apologize for being so cranky. If not, then you buy lunch."

The drive had taken nine hours, and the sun was just coming up as they parked outside the perimeter of the house and got out to look around. They had done this before and were very methodical as to how they searched an area. One walked to the left, the other to the right, intending to meet in the front of the house. Although Joe was not happy to be there, he had every intention of being thorough. He had gone about half way around when he saw something glistening in the grass. He picked it up placing it in his pocket.

Willy looked out and saw the man and woman looking around. He was tired and didn't show much interest as he went back down to "her" room. He enjoyed looking at her. He hadn't decided what to do with her, but he knew this time would be different. He laughed to himself. Killing was killing no matter how you did it! He laid down next to her, held her with one hand and held a knife in the other. It was the same knife he used to kill Jennifer. Ah, sweet Jennifer. With that thought he fell into a deep, exhausting sleep, not hearing what was going on downstairs

They met in front of the house as planned.

"Any luck?" he asked.

"No, nothing. I guess I buy you lunch."

"Maybe not." He reached into his pocket pulling out the gold object he had found. "Wasn't there some mention of a charm worn by the little girl? I found this, but it seems to be chewed up a bit."

Grace got excited and grabbed the trinket from his hand. Yes, the little girl had a charm of a poodle's head. Her mother had given it to her on her third birthday.

They walked up front and checked the door. It was locked.

"I'm going in. We have the warrant. I don't want him to get off on another technicality," she said. Standing back, Joe kicked open the rotting door.

The smell gagged them as they entered the dark hallway. Their eyes adjusted to the darkness, then they motioned to one another, pointing to the shoe marks going up the dusty stairs. They cautiously climbed up to the landing. Detective Rhymes went to the left, and Detective Sheffield went to the right, checking each room as she went. It wasn't really necessary to check each room since the footprints and smell were coming from the last door down the hall. She slowly pushed it open with her foot, gun ready.

There was the little girl lying on the bed, blood and tear stained face. And there was Willy sleeping alongside her, holding the knife in his hand. He moved slightly in his sleep.

The sound of her gun echoed through the house with its vibration, causing the dust filled room to cloud over making it difficult to see.

Joe came running down the hall, entered the room, and stood behind Grace. First he saw Willy's body lying on the floor with a bullet hole in his head then he looked over at the child who had sat up crying with outstretched arms beckoning Grace to take her. Grace dropped her gun, ran over, and clutched the child to her breast. She looked over at Joe's stricken face. In a slow, sobbing whisper, she said, "I couldn't let him do this again."

The official record was that Willy resisted arrest, and Detective Sheffield shot in self-defense. Detective Rhyme's report backed up her story.

2
LIFE'S LAST JOURNEY

"<u>Life is a journey</u> that must be traveled no matter how bad the roads and accommodations."

"Death is part of that journey and can only be traveled alone."

December 20th

It was his last run. He had been driving these big rigs for over 40 years, taking the holiday run since he had no family to share the holidays with. Orphaned at age seven, he never had a "permanent" family, especially during the holidays. Why should this year be any different? His run would take him approximately four days. He was getting too old for this sort of job, the bouncing of the cab making his back ache and kidneys fail. Yes, this was his last run. What he would do next, he didn't know. He had enough money saved to live well and take a vacation once or twice a year. He didn't particularly like his apartment, so perhaps he would relocate. He'd make new friends and do things he always wanted to do…

Who was he kidding? He had no desire to start over in a new location, and he didn't care too much about making new friends. He grabbed the handle and boosted himself up into the cab seat, checked his log, started the engine, and off he went.

She was running late. Every year, it took her longer and longer to get ready. For the third time, she checked her notebook. She had packed enough clothes to last one week, enough money to pay all her expenses and a little extra for a few more gifts for the children: a little scarf, a book, candy, just something to brighten their faces for what should be a happy time of year.

…Where were her keys? Her mind must be going—she couldn't even remember where she placed the keys for the rental car. Found them!

"Now, have I forgotten anything?" She looked around. She was ready. She wouldn't be returning to her apartment of 23 years. All her precious belongings were given away or shipped to a local thrift shop. It should take her four days to reach her destination. The car was already loaded. She got in, started the engine and off she went.

December 21st

On the second day of his run, the weather began to change; not quite cold enough for snow, but cold enough to have to defrost the windows, put on an extra pair of socks, and keep the heater running. He would stop and get a hot coffee at his next stop. He turned on the radio to listen to the updated weather forecast—it wasn't good. His journey might take longer than he expected.

She should have known she would forget something. She was told to bring the car in for an oil change before she left. Now the car seemed to be acting funny. Only a woman who knew nothing about cars would describe it that way. Well, it WAS acting funny! She needed to stop at the next station and have a mechanic take a look. Her journey would have to take a detour. Weather was getting cold. She could sure use a hot cup of coffee.

There wasn't much room in the lot for his big rig. He supposed everyone had the same idea—a nice hot cup of coffee does a body good. He pulled around back, locked up, and walked behind the other vehicles to the front. By the time he entered the small diner, his fingers were freezing, ears and nose bright red. He reached into his coat pocket for a crumpled napkin and wiped his nose. The place was packed. Down at the end of the counter was an empty seat. He started to walk down but was not quite quick enough.

A young woman got to the seat ahead of him. Well, maybe not quite so young—about mid-fifties, 5'5" with dirty blonde hair. She seemed in a hurry. No, not so much in a hurry as upset. Oh well, he would just have to stand and drink his coffee and wait for another available seat. As he ordered his coffee and muffin he could hear the woman on her cell phone. He hated those things. It was such a nuisance having to listen to everyone's conversation. Why did people feel they had to speak so loud?

"I don't think I can be there in time," she said. "Something's wrong with my car, and because of the holiday, they can't get the parts for a few days. No, I'm in the middle of nowhere, no trains, busses, not even another rent-a-car. I'm not even sure if there is a place for me to stay the night. Come to think of it, I probably don't even have enough money to carry me through for an extra few days. Oh, what am I to do? What about the children? I have everything packed in my car."

Although he felt sorry for her, he didn't want to get involved. This was his last run. He didn't want anything to complicate things, but the more he listened to her tale of woe, the more he felt inclined to offer some assistance. Perhaps he could offer to pay for her coffee. *Oh, big spender! Here she is stranded, and I offer her a cup of coffee…*

Before he knew what he was saying…

"Excuse me, I couldn't help but overhear your conversation. I'm heading west, and if you're going that way, perhaps you'd like to hitch a ride?" As soon as he said it, he thought he must be crazy offering her a ride.

"That's very kind of you, but what would I do with my car?"

"You can leave it at the mechanics and pick it up on your way back. Where are you headed?"

Surprised at his kindness, she avoided his question.

"I can't expect you to go to all that trouble, you know, the holidays and all."

"I wouldn't have offered if I didn't feel I could handle it. As I said, I'm heading west so if you're heading anywhere in that direction, we can have our coffee, load you up, and off we go."

She was hesitant, but since she didn't have too many options— none, actually—she took him up on his offer. She had nothing to lose, and he seemed so kind. He drove her to the station and parked as close to her car as he could. It had started to sleet.

"Where exactly are you headed?" she asked.

"I'm heading for Twin Falls, Idaho. I have a few deliveries to make on the way, and if the weather holds up, I should be there by Christmas. I usually stay overnight to do a personal errand then head back home. We could pick your car up on our way back."

She tried to keep her hands from shaking, keep the shock from her face. She wondered how he knew she was going to Twin Falls? Did he hear her say something over the phone? He seemed honest enough. What did he mean by on OUR way back? All this was running through her mind when he opened the door for her. She got out and ran over to the car. Ice had formed around the lock. She couldn't get the key in. Snow was now covering the ground, about an inch high. She ran back to the truck and knocked on the door. He opened the window.

"I have several things in the trunk that have to go with me. Can you help me put them in the back of the truck?"

This was getting worse and worse as time went on. He was beginning to regret ever having offered her any help. In all his runs, he never picked up a rider and now he picked up a damsel

...distress that seemed not to have a brain in her head. He got out of the cab and took the keys. Snow was falling harder as he walked over to her car. Luckily, the lock on the trunk was not yet frozen. He opened the trunk. He couldn't believe his eyes. Packages. Holiday wrapped packages. All shapes and sizes. He looked over at her standing in the snow, shivering. She looked so pitiful. She gave him a smile. A smile that, had it not been so cold, would have melted his heart.

What did I get myself into? he thought. He waved her over, and they began to empty her trunk and placed the packages into the truck. They got in and off they went.

What a journey this is going to be... they both thought. Little did they know, this would be a journey of a life time.

It took a while for the cab to get warm, snow now falling hard against the window and covering the road. Both driver and passenger remained silent, not knowing what to say. She was nervous, and he was concentrating on the icy road.

"Well, I suppose after all you have done for me, I should introduce myself. I'm Catherine Hall." She put out her hand and realized it was a stupid gesture since he had all he could do to control the sliding truck with both hands. He turned his head for a quick moment and smiled.

"I'm Jarrod Price, people call me Jake. You can turn on the radio and try to get some music, although I'm not sure what kind of reception you'll get with this weather. Where are you headed?"

She didn't quite know what to say. It was hard to believe that two total strangers would be beaded for the same place. "Actually, I'm also headed for Twin Falls. I go there every Christmas. I only managed to go about 150 miles before I started to have car trouble."

"That explains all the gifts. You must have a large family. Personally, I never celebrate the holidays. Fact of the matter is, I don't have any family. Christmas is just another day." Conversation was smooth and uncommonly comfortable with an ease that only comes from years of friendship. Time passed quickly, and before they knew it, it was time for dinner. "I usually drive until about 8:00, then eat and settle in for the night, but if you are hungry now, we can stop and look for a place to stay later. It's too cold to sleep in the cab," he said.

She was thankful for that. Actually, she had never slept with a man, and she could not imagine sleeping in such close quarters with a man she just met.

"Jake, I'm not really hungry just yet, and since the snow seems to have let up a bit, if you aren't too tired, we could go on a bit more."

They drove for another 100 miles before the snow started up again. He pulled over and drove behind a motel with a small restaurant attached. Admittedly, it was a bit seedy, but due to the present road conditions he felt it best to get a room before there were no more vacancies.

"Is this okay with you, Catherine? I'm not sure what's up ahead. I'm usually far passed this part of the trip before I start looking for a room."

When she didn't answer, he looked over and saw that she had fallen asleep. She looked so peaceful now, not as she had at the diner. She was beautiful, he thought. Once again, he wondered what possessed him to offer her a ride.

"Catherine? We're at the motel." He nudged her gently, and her eyes opened, slowly, looked around until their eyes met and she smiled. "I'll just get your bag, and we'll go check in."

"Oh NO! In all the confusion and moving all the packages out of the trunk I forgot to get my suitcase from the back seat. I don't have any clothes or toiletries!" Tears started to fall down her cheek, and the quiver in her voice made her sound like a child.

"I'm sure the hotel has some *toiletries*, whatever they are, and I have a couple of clean shirts I could lend you. We're bound to come across a general store tomorrow. Don't get so upset. Worse things can happen."

"How can you be so calm after driving all day, picking up a perfect stranger, and having to listen to my babbling for hours on end?"

"Who said you were perfect?" he replied with a boyish grin. She looked at him with question in her eyes. He was smiling, trying to make a joke. He was trying to make the best of a terrible situation.

As luck would have it, there were two rooms left, and the hotel clerk had an extra toothbrush and toothpaste and lotion. Sure enough, his shirt made a perfect night shirt, and after a long, hot bath she fell asleep.

December 22nd

When he woke the next morning, he could see driving would not be easy. There were snow drifts three feet high, and it was still coming down. Roads had been cleared, but black ice would be a problem. He called ahead to say travel would be slow going and he would be late. He did not, however, tell them about his unexpected passenger. If he was going to make any headway, they had better get started. He dialed her room. When she answered, he said, "It's 7:30, rise and shine. Meet me in the coffee shop in 15 minutes. We have to get going." Then he hung up and went out to check on the truck and gas up. The snow was higher than he thought, and it took him some time to do his checklist and enter into his travel log the amount of miles he had traveled. They were just a little past Des Moines. At this rate, it would take him much longer than planned. He had to make it to Idaho in time.

She didn't exactly appreciate being woken up so early and certainly didn't appreciate his abruptness shouting orders at her. She got out of bed and looked out the window.

"God, no. How can he possibly drive in all that snow? No wonder his voice was so harsh!"

She quickly washed up and put on his other shirt with her

jeans, packed up her few things, and off to the coffee shop she went. By the time she got there, she was covered with snow. She ordered for both of them to save time then made a call explaining she would be late, but she promised to be there before Christmas. She just had to be in Idaho on time.

By the time he entered the small diner, he was covered with snow with ice forming on his eyebrows. He looked almost like a half-made snowman as he walked up to the booth, grabbing the hot coffee as he sat down. She began to laugh mischievously.

"And just what seems to be so funny, little lady?" he asked.

She was still laughing when she replied, "You should see yourself, snow all over you."

"In case you haven't noticed, it is snowing out. And if you think it's so funny, then perhaps tomorrow morning you can get up at 6:00 a.m., check the truck and clean off all the windows! I'm freezing. I think I must have left my gloves at the coffee shop yesterday. My fingers are about to fall off."

"Oh, poor man. I have a pair of mittens you can use. They're old but warm." She went rummaging through her pocketbook and pulled out a pink and white polka dot pair of mittens and handed them to him.

He looked at her as if she were stark raving mad.

"No thanks, I think I'll let the fingers fall where they will."

"Okay, see if I care," she answered.

"Well, if my fingers do fall off, you can always drive the truck!"

"No, Jake, I don't know how to drive a truck. I can barely drive my car! Please don't expect me to..." She looked up and he was smiling.

"I'm only joking. Don't take things so seriously. Drink up! We have to get going."

Before long, they were on their way. As they traveled west, the roads began to clear, and temperatures rose above freezing. Hopefully, they would be able to make 400 miles before having to stop for the night.

"I believe there is a Walmart up ahead," he said. "We could stop, have a bite to eat and you can pick up your toiletries or whatever and stretch our legs a bit."

"Well, Jake, I'll say one thing for you—you take me only to the-best of places!"

They laughed as he pulled into a space big enough for the truck. He got out and opened the door for her. He may not take her to the best places, but he was always a gentleman. She made her purchases, including a new pair of gloves for him. After all, it was the least she could do for him after all he was doing for her. As they sat in the small section designated for shoppers to eat a fast food lunch, they said very little, yet there was no silence. It was as if they read each other's minds, and there was no need for words.

When they were finished, he asked, "Would you like to take a walk? There is a nice park with a little pond out back, and it should be beautiful all covered with snow."

"I'd love to. Let me just put on my hat and mittens." She paused, reached into the bag with her purchases and pulled out a pair of black, fur lined, leather gloves and handed them to him. "I'd hate to see your fingers fall off, and even more so, I'd hate to have to drive the truck."

He took the gloves from her hands and put them on. He bent down and gave her a feather light kiss on the cheek.

"Thank you, Catherine."

She knew then that taking this journey with him was a big mistake. She was falling in love with this stranger. This stranger she knew nothing about; and even worse, he knew nothing about her.

On their walk through the park, he felt a bond was beginning to form between them. They talked about nothing important, but as they talked, something stronger than friendship was beginning to form. It was a nice feeling. A feeling he never had before. She would stop and take pictures of snow drifts against a tree with icicles glistening in the sun. She seemed so happy doing such simple things, and he was happy just watching her.

Around 8:00, they arrived in Scotts Bluff, said their goodnights, and arranged to meet at 7:00 a.m. for breakfast.

December 23rd

Both were up bright and early and were eating breakfast when she asked, "What are you going to do when we get to Twin Falls? For Christmas, I mean?"

"I have some personal business to attend to. It doesn't take me long. I'll be ready to head back by early afternoon. If you are coming back with me, then I suppose I could leave a little later, after you finish delivering all your presents."

She looked at him sadly, grateful for the consideration.

"I only have one stop. Perhaps you would like to join me in the morning, then we could have lunch before you go on your way."

He didn't catch the "you" instead of "we." He wished he could be with her for the holiday. He had never spent the holiday with anyone special before. He never answered her. He just looked away.

Minutes later, he broke the uncomfortable silence.

"Let's take a detour, just a little out of our way off Highway 85. There's a little place just outside of here called Hawk Springs. We could go to the Hawk Springs Recreation Area. I bet you can get some great pictures there."

Although she was excited about the prospect of getting more pictures, she replied, "Are you sure? Don't we have a schedule to keep? Don't you have to be someplace?"

"Yes, I do, but it won't take us much out of the way, and I promise I'll only let you take one roll of film then we have to go."

Her laugh was so loud, it startled him.

"Where have you been? Cameras are digital now, no film."

Before she knew it, they were entering the recreation area, and sure enough, there were plenty of things for her to take pictures of. As they walked further into the park, Jake stopped suddenly and pointed to the left. There, amidst some fir trees, was a group of elk trying to get some morsel of food from under the snow. She started snapping pictures, walking around the mounds of snow.

He watched her. A larger, more majestic elk stood off to the side overseeing his domain. He was beautiful but not as beautiful as the woman he watched. He motioned to her and pointed to the magnificent creature. She turned but instead of taking pictures of the elk, she snapped several of Jake looking at her, smiling.

"Your time is up, we have to get going."

"Not yet," she begged. "I—" Before she could finish what she was about to say, Jake threw a snowball at her landing right on her shoulder making her drop the camera. "Why you awful man!"

She bent over, pretending to pick up her camera but instead made a snowball of her own and took aim…

POW! Right on his head!

He ran up and pulled her to him and held her tight. He didn't want to let her go, and she didn't want him to, either.

It was almost time to pull over for the night when he saw a huge sign on the side of the road — ALL CHRISTMAS TREES $10. He swung the rig over to the side of the road.

"I'll be right back."

In a flash, he was out of the cab, and before she knew it, he had loaded up the biggest tree in the lot and was ready to go.

"What was that all about?" she asked.

"Just something I had to do," he replied with a devilishly wide grin.

December 24th

If all went well and the snow held off, they would reach the Grand Tetons today. They might not reach their destination on Christmas Eve as planned, but they certainly would be there for Christmas.

"You know, Jake, I don't understand. You delivered all your merchandise and yet you traveled hundreds of miles beyond that point. What takes you so much out of your way?"

"Catherine," he said softly with a tenderness she had not heard before, "I don't have family of my own, and I don't want to be in my apartment alone during the holidays. I'd rather be on the road. Besides, there is one place I like to visit this time of year, so I drive a little farther to complete my journey."

She was quiet for a moment before she said, "I'm glad I got to know you, and I'm glad we got to spend this time with one another. If we are a little ahead of schedule, would you mind stopping at a department store? I forgot one present. It won't take me long. I know exactly what I want."

The day passed quickly, and the weather only just started to snow shortly before they had to stop for the night.

"Well, Catherine, this is Christmas Eve. Want to go down to the rest stop for a beer?"

The smile on her face made his heart jump.

"I don't drink beer but a nice hot cup of tea would be nice."

The evening was a pleasant one with lively chatter and laughing. It had been a wonderful day, but the real Jake and Catherine were never revealed. Each had a journey—separate from the other.

December 25th

The following morning, they were loaded and ready to go by 6:00 a.m. They were silent most of the way, only speaking occasionally. Before they knew it, they saw signs for Twin Falls.

"I'm going to park the truck over at the filling station. I should be done with my business by noon, but I can wait for you at the diner on Center Street until you are ready to head back. Don't hurry. I can always take a nap in the truck or have another cup of coffee."

She looked up at him and placed her hand on the side of his face. It felt so warm on his skin. He reached up and took hold of her hand.

"What's wrong?" he asked.

"Jake, I won't be returning with you. My journey with you is over." She reached down and picked up a small package and handed it to him. "Merry Christmas."

He didn't question her about not returning with him. After all, he hardly knew her. He squeezed her hand then let it fall to her side. He turned and walked away. It wasn't until he had completely turned away that she let the tears fall from her eyes and down her face.

On the other side of town, there stood a church. Old, sadly in need for repair but decorated for the holidays, welcoming everyone who passed to take a look and admire. To its side was an even older building with a sign over the door that was so worn you could hardly read it — *Twin Falls Light of Day Orphanage.* Catherine had been here many times before. She came here every Christmas. Catherine sat on the floor with the children, making ornaments for the tree that Santa was expected to bring at any moment. Their hands were busy cutting, gluing, and stringing popcorn. Their laughter was contagious. This was the one thing that brought joy to her life. This was her last visit here. Sickness had taken over her body. Seeing the children so happy was why she traveled so far. She stood up pretending to hear something.

"Listen, children," she said. "Do you hear that? I think Santa is coming."

Just then, sure enough, through the front door came the biggest, most jovial Santa carrying the tallest, most beautiful tree she had ever seen. While the older children decorated the tree, Santa put each small child on his knee and listened while they told him what they wanted for Christmas. He laughed when they pulled his beard, was patient when they cried and hugged them when they told him they loved him. When the tree was finished, Catherine placed all the packages she brought under the tree.

"Miss Catherine!" one of the children shouted. "Tell Santa what you want for Christmas." They pushed her up the stairs until she was forced to sit on his lap. She was laughing so hard she didn't notice the look of surprise on Santa's face.

"And what pretty lady do you want for Christmas?"

"I don't want to be alone this Christmas. I want to stay right here."

When the cookies and soda were finished and Santa on his way, she took her coat and headed for the church. What a wonderful day it had been. Waiting outside was Jake. He walked up to her and grabbed her hand.

"What were you doing here?" he asked.

"I come here every year. This is where I grew up. I don't understand. How did you know I was here?" she asked.

He smiled, took the Santa beard out of his coat pocket, placed it on his face and said loudly "HO, HO, HO! I'm Santa, and I want to grant you your wish."

She was quiet for a moment, and with tears in her eyes, she looked up.

"Jake, this will be my last Christmas. I can't expect you to stay with me."

"I don't have to be anywhere I don't want to be, and I want to be with you."

"But why?"

"This is the orphanage I grew up in. This is the only family I ever knew. I come here every year to play Santa, but usually come on Christmas Eve. This year, because of the storm, I was late. I had a wonderful drive out here with you. I don't want to end it now." He held her tight, not wanting to let her go.

"We had a wonderful journey, but now I have my own journey to take, a journey I alone can take." She stood on her tip toes and kissed him. Then she walked away.

December 26th

He drove back slowly over the icy roads—alone. He missed her. He looked over on the seat beside him. There was the small, gaily wrapped package she had given him. He pulled the truck over and turned off the engine letting the snow cover the windshield. He reached over for the package and gently opened it.

Inside was a round, musical snow globe with two people holding hands standing around a Christmas tree. He shook it letting the enclosed snow swirl around the couple as he slowly wound it up and listened to the music.

Somewhere down this road
I know someone's waiting
Years of dreams just can't be wrong.
Arms will open wide
I'll be safe and wanted finally home where I belong.
*Heart, I'm trusting you on this journey.**

3
LOVE IS STRANGE

Annette sat at the table she usually took every day. She kept to herself most of the time but enjoyed her daily outings to the restaurant where she ate her breakfast, read the morning paper, and enjoyed looking around and hearing news about the community. Annette lived in a silent world, so the term "hearing" didn't actually apply to her. She chose this particular table since it afforded her a perfect view of everyone in the restaurant. She could read lips, sometimes learning the darkest of secrets of her fellow diners. People considered her the **"fruitcake"** of the town. That didn't really bother her since she supposed that was a nicer term other than "crazy."

On this particular day, she took note of a couple sitting in the corner (the best table for observing people) obviously very much in love. They were holding hands and laughing.

"I'll tell you a secret: I love chocolate," the woman said to her companion. She smiled up at him and he took her hand and brought it up to his lips and kissed it.

"Can I get you more coffee?" The waitress interrupted her spying. Although she did not hear what was asked, she noticed the hot pot of coffee in the waitress's hand hovering over her coffee cup. Annette waved her away just as a mother and her two children sat at the table directly in front, almost obscuring her view of the woman.

"We could get lost in Canada very easily." The man spoke now. Annette could see that he was becoming agitated. The woman was beginning to cry.

Lost! Why would anyone want to get lost in Canada? She wondered. *Too cold for my liking… Damn. I wish those kids would sit down and eat. Why do they have to keep bobbing up and down?*

Giving up trying to keep up with the couple's conversation, she started to read her paper. Suddenly, out of the corner of her eye she saw the woman abruptly rise from the table.

"God, I'm telling you, he has come back to haunt me."

"Sit down, people are watching. I don't like to be made a fool of."

"They can't hear us."

"Sit."

The woman sat as ordered. Their talk had taken an unpleasant turn. Oh, if she had only been able to view the entire conversation.

She looked over at another table in the center, where four women were intently discussing something. At that point, one of the children, a little boy, threw a toy across the room landing on their table. Fury crossed their faces as one of the women picked up the toy and returned it to the child. The mother thanked her and proceeded to scold the child.

The woman returned to her table and said: *"Now you know why I despise kids."*

They laughed and one added, *"He should be thrown in a hole."*

"Sure," said the woman, *"and if the hole is deep enough, no one will ever find him."*

Annette didn't like kids either, but throwing them in a hole was a bit extreme. By the looks of these women, they were probably the original woman's libbers of the sixties burning their bras in protest. Having been reprimanded, the children were now sitting quietly, and she could once again see the couple sitting in the corner. They were calmer now, more "lovey-dovey," but what she saw next didn't make any sense.

"The whole thing doesn't make any sense. Haunting someone to death is ridiculous." The woman shook her head.

Annette was startled.

What in the world are they talking about? Hauntings? And they call me a "fruitcake." Those people are really crazy. She strained her eyes, trying to make out the rest of the conversation. Their lips were no longer clearly visible since their heads were so close together, whispering so that no one could hear.

The waitress came back with the check. Annette, not wanting to leave, ordered another cup of coffee. The waitress turned, cursed, knowing Annette could not hear, "Damn, couldn't you have taken the coffee before, so I didn't have to make another trip? My feet are killing me."

The woman sat back in her chair and said, smiling, *"I don't care what you think. Everyone is entitled to their own opinion."*

He smiled back.

"You're looking at it from only a woman's point of view. I'm telling you, from a man's point of view, that was the worst (indistinguishable word) I ever saw."

Of course, she's looking at it from a woman's point of view—she's a woman, you jerk.

The waitress poured her another cup of coffee. By this time, the mother and her children were gone, and her view of the entire restaurant was unobscured. She looked over at the four women who were still talking. The same woman who returned the toy to the child got up and walked over to the couple sitting in the corner.

"I'm sorry, but we could not help but overhear your conversation." She then leaned over and directed her comment to the man, startled by the intrusion. *"For your Information, from a woman's point of view, that was the best James Bond*

movie I ever saw." *She then turned to the woman and said,* "*And if you go with him to Canada, I assure you, then you will not only be haunted by the memory of your late husband but by the fact you made one big mistake.*"

She walked away from the couple and returned to her friends, who were paying the bill and getting ready to leave. A few grumbles came from the back of the room, but Annette could not see anyone due to the darkness in the corner.

Annette sat with her mouth opened. Boy, she must have missed a lot of the conversation due to those mischievous kids. The couple, still in shock, prepared to leave. She might as well leave, too. As she gathered up her belongings, she glanced over to the far left of the room, now lit by sun coming from behind a cloud through the window. Two men in dark suits sat having a drink. One man said to the other, "*Boy, that bitch is a piece of work. If she were my wife I'd give her a good beating.*"

The other man turned his head and said, "*Forget the beating, a knife would do the job but a gun would be cleaner.*"

The first man then put his hand in his jacket and lifted something from his pocket that looked like the handle of a gun. "*Then I have just the thing to do the job right!*"

Annette quickly sat back down and ordered yet another cup of coffee.

"Now, this is starting to get interesting."

4
STATUE OF STONE

Carolena sat at her window high in the tower overlooking the sea. Although she had access to all the information she needed, the only thing she wanted was denied her: Companionship.

Her dreams at night were dreams of sadness, dreams making her frightened of the loneliness she experienced every day. But now, as she looked out over the water, her daydreams were tranquil, full of hope.

BANG! BANG, BANG!

The noise startled her yet exhilarated her. Someone was bringing food, her only contact with the outside. She quickly got up and ran to open the door. To her surprise, there stood a young woman, much her same size and age. Her name was Madelana. Madelana placed the tray on the table, smiled, and started to leave.

"Oh, please don't go. Stay with me awhile until I am done with my meal, then you can take it away and not have to make the long trip back up the tower."

And so it began…

Every night, Madelana would come and sit with Carolena, and they would talk of many things. She told her of how her father kept her hidden away until he felt there was a man most suitable and worthy of her hand in marriage.

"Why?" Madelana asked. "How can you know who is most suitable unless you have seen the world?"

They began to form a plan.

Carolena's hair was long, the color of golden wheat that flowed behind her as she walked. Unlike in the fairytale of Rapunzel, her hair was not long enough to allow her to climb down or anyone to climb up into the tower. So Madelana purchased a long rope.

Once Carolena got the knack of climbing, she was able to scale the tower in no time at all. Madelana would wait in the tower until Carolena was on the ground then lift the rope and wait for her return just before daybreak then she would put the rope down, so that Carolena could climb back up.

Carolena loved her freedom and the feel of sand beneath her feet. She explored the grounds, wandering through the gardens and winding paths beyond the castle. One night, she came across a statue of a man placed in a garden of roses.

"My handsome man of stone, you are as isolated here as I am in my tower. If only you could be the suitable one my father searches for."

Every night, Carolena would come and talk to her statue. He became her friend, the object of her dreams, and more importantly, her lover. One night, she became so lost in her thought, she hadn't noticed the sun was already up. She scurried from the garden, leaving the beach and statue behind. Up the rope she climbed, entering, once again, her dark and dusty room. It was late, and Madelana had to go. In her haste she forgot to lift the rope.

Carolena laid in bed and heard a great commotion outside the tower. She looked over at the window and saw the rope still outside. She ran over but it was too late, one of her father's security guards was pulling the rope away from the wall. She could see he was angry, but as she looked across the yard, she saw more than anger on her father's face. She saw betrayal and even worse, hatred.

Madelana was no longer allowed to bring Carolena her meals. Her socks were taken away, and her father forbade her monthly outings. She became more obsessed, thinking of her statue, her lover. If she really used her imagination, she could see him in the garden below.

One night, there was a cool breeze, and the waves of the sea beckoned her to come and run in the sand. She saw his outstretched hand. She sat by the windowsill, watching the birds of the night fly silently in the sky, swooping in and out of the water.

He's calling me, she thought. She became dizzy and fell to the garden below.

The next day, the alarm sounded. Carolena was not in her room. Her father and all the security men looked everywhere and sent search parties to neighboring villages to find her. She was never found.

But curiously, while searching, they noticed that the statue in the garden was also missing, and they found two sets of footprints in the sand leading out to sea.

5

A BOY NAMED JASON

He sat waiting in a crouched position, knees and back hurting. The boy would be out soon, always coming out to play around this time. He was anxious and began biting his nails. He had done this before and had little of his nails left to bite. Damn, someone was coming.

He stood up quickly and walked towards the stranger.

"Hey, pal," he said nervously. "I just moved in two blocks over, #218. My dog ran out while the movers were doing their thing. A brown and white mutt, about 50 pounds. If you happen to see her, can you let me know? No phone yet."

"Sure thing, pal, my name is Mark," the stranger said, extending his hand, "just moved in myself this weekend."

He didn't offer his hand or a name, just turned and walked away.

She was in a hurry, not looking where she was going. She hadn't slept well for several nights. Dreams (more like nightmares) kept haunting her sleep. She felt something then looked down. There stood a homeless boy pulling on her coattail. She pulled her coat and continued on her way without saying a word.

He was a small boy, not even three feet tall, age could not be determined due to the amount of decomposition of the body. Identity unknown. The age and who he was may not be known, but it was

28

evident that he did not die a painless death, and when death did come,
it was a blessing.
A man stood in the distant shadows.

They sat across from each other. Detective Green leaned back in his chair with a notebook propped up on his lap, pen in hand. She sat stiff, waiting for another question.

"So you claim to have dreamt about a boy…a dead boy… then you claim to have seen not only him in the park but also who you think was his murderer in this dream?"

"Yes." She could see he wasn't paying attention. He was doodling on the pad instead of taking notes.

"Can you describe the person you believe to be the murderer?"

"No, but I'm sure I could recognize him, if I saw him."

Detective Green was getting a bit agitated. He thought he was dealing with a real nut case. He shouldn't think like that. There was a time when people thought he was a little crazy, too.

"I'll have my secretary bring in some mug shots for you to look at and…how old did you say you thought the boy was?"

"Well, it's hard to say, but I think around six."

"I'll also have her bring in some photos of missing boys for your review, but without knowing about when he disappeared, it's going to be hard." He left the room and spoke to his secretary. "Bring her the mug shots and missing children files." He leaned over and whispered, "She'll get tired of looking in about an hour. Keep an eye on her. See you later."

Detective Green returned four hours later to find her still sitting in his office going through stacks and stacks of files.

"You're still looking?"

"Yes, I still have several to go."

"Don't bother with any more today. Go home and let's see what we come up with."

She was being dismissed. He didn't believe her to begin with, why should he now?

Dreaming. Restless. Focus. Try to focus. A child running, pulling at my coattail. Someone running after him. Concentrate on his face. Vaguely familiar. I just can't seem to focus…

A scar, on the right side of his face. Whose face?

He had worked hard to find him after they moved away. When he finally did find the boy, he was overjoyed. It was easier to grab him than he ever imagined. The boy was so trusting. The mere mention of going to the circus was enough to get him in the van. Only a small dose of chloroform was necessary to make his small body go limp and silent. The shack was only a two-hour ride away. Then all this waiting would be worth it.

He brought him in the shack and tied him up and waited for him to wake. What he would do then caused her dream to become a nightmare. How long he would keep the boy alive, she didn't know. She knew he would kill again.

"Detective Green, I know this is very strange to you. Hell, it's strange to me. I've never had this happen before, and I certainly don't want it to happen again. I think the murderer had a scar. Surely you must be able to break down our search now that we know he has a scar on his face."

"Miss Wellers…"

"Ms. Wellerton," she corrected.

"Yes, sorry. This is not 'our' search. We don't even know if the face you imagine you saw is even the face of a murderer. I'm sorry, we just don't have the manpower to continue investigating what you *think* might be more than a dream."

"But what about the…?"

"Please, enough is enough. If you come across some concrete evidence, give me a call." As he got up from his desk, surprise registered on her face. "What is it now, Ms. Wellerton?"

"I just noticed you have a small scar on your face."

"So now you suspect me. Really, enough!"

She left the room and walked down the hall to the elevator. While waiting, Detective Green's secretary joined her.

"Hello Ms. Wellerton. Back looking over some photos?"

"No, your boss doesn't seem to think it would do any good. How long have you worked for him?"

She thought for a moment.

"I guess about five and a half years. He came to LA from Chicago shortly after the disappearance of his son. It was the only case he was never able to solve. Had a nervous breakdown, they say. Seems to be okay now though. He never talks about it, like it never happened. He's a tough boss, but he does a good job. Sorry he was not more cooperative with you."

They both entered the elevator and remained silent.

The same boy tugged at her coattail. He looked up, sadness on his face.

"What do you want from me?" she asked.

He handed her a key with a nametag attached and walked away. The tag read "Jason."

She saw a man, something in his hand…

A gun? Tears fall from his face.

She woke from her dream. This time, however, she was not frightened. The boy was trying to tell her something. She spent the better part of the following day at the library, trying to find listings of missing boys named Jason. No luck. She then expanded her search to boys missing in the Chicago area. There was one listing: Jason Green, age six.

"Detective Green I've had another dream. This time the boy gave me his name."

The detective gave a sigh, put down his pen and looked up.

"Please don't tell me his name was Rumpelstiltskin!"

"No," she replied in a steady voice, "and I resent your flippant attitude."

He clutched his desk, rage overtaking his thoughts as he stood with a menacing look on his face.

"What do you really want? Who are you, a reporter?"

"No, I'm not a reporter. I just want to find out what happened to a poor little boy that seems to be reaching out to me—from wherever—for help. He told me his name was Jason. I think, somehow, you can help me more than I can help you."

He sat down, crushed with emotion.

"I'm sure there is no connection, but my son was named Jason. He went missing about 10 years ago. I was taken off the case, but the investigators in charge were never able to find my son. After the case was closed, I started looking on my own but ended up having a breakdown. I may have had to give up, but I'll never forget him."

"I'm sorry, but if you can tell me more about the case then perhaps I can help. I must be having these dreams for a reason."

"Forget it. For me, the case must remain closed. Otherwise, I'll end up…" Sadness swept over him. He was done talking.

Several weeks passed with no further dreams. She made a few more trips to the library gathering information, but none of importance until one day, in an old book store, she came across a Chicago newspaper with a front page heading "Search for Jason at an End." It stated that the son of Detective Green had been abducted from their new Chicago home. Police questioned former neighbors, and the new resident, Mr. Mark Clark, stated a strange man had claimed to be searching for his missing dog in their backyard. It was said that the man acted oddly when he heard that the Greens had moved away. Further investigation revealed that a small, decomposed body of a boy was found in an old shack off Highway 34. However, Detective Green was unable to identify the body as his son. Although the search had now stopped, the case would remain open in the event new evidence materialized.

She awoke with a start. She was just about to get a glimpse of the person running after the boy. It was raining now, thunder, lightning. She drifted back to sleep.

The lightening lit up the field, casting long shadows of darkness. A man stood by an old shack, breathless. He held a shovel in one hand and a cigarette in the other. The smell of smoke filled her nostrils, a sweet smell. A mound of dirt was piled high against the side of the structure. It was time to dispose of the body. The boy was of no use to him now that he was dead. The man looks towards the door of the shack. As he turned his head, she got a quick glance of his face. White, madness in his dark eyes, a scar…

He heard a sound inside the shack and walked towards the shack and entered. A crushing sound, then silence.

Detective Green continued the search even after he was taken off the case. The other detectives had kept him informed and shared the various leads with him until one day they had to admit they had to close the case. He continued to follow various leads until one day he read that a mysterious man was seen supposedly searching for his dog. One clue led to the other, and one day, he spotted a man with a slight scar on the right side of his face. He followed him: Detective Green watched as the man dug the hole. Cautiously, he moved to the back of the shack and entered the rear window. He saw the mangled body of a boy on the floor and began to lose control. That could not be Jason, his little boy, the joy of his life; the condition of his body unrecognizable. He stumbled over a basket set on the floor, striking his cheek on an exposed nail. What happened next left his mind forever.

The man entered the shack and looked right into the eyes of Detective Green so full of rage that he was unable to control himself, and urine ran down his leg causing a puddle around his feet. He was kicked in one swift, violent movement and thrown through the window with bits and pieces of glass entering his face and body. The detective exited the shack and pulled out a gun and pumped every bullet into the man. Tears ran down his face. He picked up the shovel, piercing his body over and over until all his strength was spent. Calmly, he kicked the body into the hole and buried him in the hell in which he deserved. Without looking back, he left that place, his son, and all memory of what had happened.

He spent the next several months in an institution for the insane. Someone had found the body of a boy thought to be Jason, but his father was unable to recognize him. Whether that was due to the decomposition of the body or denial no one knew.

She dressed and had a cup of coffee. She knew the truth now. Would it do any good to tell Detective Green about her dream? What difference would it make? Jason's murderer could do no further harm. Detective Green had suffered enough. She took a slow walk to the police station. She walked up to Detective Green's office and asked his secretary if she could see him.

"What now, Ms. Wellerton?"

"I just wanted you to know that the dreams I was having seem to have stopped. I feel that the reason for those dreams has been fulfilled."

"And why do you think that?"

She looked right into his sad, vacant eyes and said, "I think the little boy is finally at peace now, and I am going to tell the police to go to a little shack about two hours from here and in a deep hole alongside of the shack, where they will find his murderer. It's the same shack they found the body of a small boy named Jason."

34

6

A FRIEND FOR THE HOLIDAY

"I told you. I have an important appointment today, and I can't get out of my drive. You said you would be here shortly. That was over three hours ago."

"Sir, I told you we would get someone there as soon as possible. I never…"

"Don't tell me that. I have to get out of my driveway, and there is no way I can shovel two feet of snow by myself."

"We are doing the best we…"

"Don't give me excuses. If you couldn't get here, you should have just said so. Now it is too late for me to make another appointment. I need someone here NOW."

"I'm sorry, sir. We just can't get to everyone at once. Please be…"

He never let her finish. He slammed the phone down, cracking the headpiece. He'd shovel himself out, and the hell with them. He shouldn't get all excited. After all, he had a bad heart, and this type of excitement was not good for him. For that matter, shoveling the snow wouldn't be good for him either. He didn't really have an appointment, and in truth, it wasn't as if he had holiday shopping to do, he had no family, and his friends…well, he no longer had any. He'd take his time and shovel away the snow that had accumulated in drifts up against his house. Despite the rise in temperature, another storm was due the next day.

He went to the front closet and put on his heavy boots, vest, hat, jacket, scarf, and a pair of warm gloves. He put a pair of mittens over the gloves and then went through the garage grabbing a snow shovel on his way out. The glitter of snow sparkled in the sun. He looked around. No one else was bothering to brave the cold and shovel snow. Was he crazy?

SPLAT!—a snowball struck him in the small of his back.

"What the h—!" He looked around again as he shook the snow from his coat. No sign of anyone.

SPLAT!—this time, he turned quickly and faced what he thought was the direction of the attack. He saw something, but…

He took a closer look. Just a headless snowman on his neighbor's front lawn.

Boy, he thought, *someone must have been up pretty early.*

The snowman was about five feet tall, heavy on the bottom, round in the middle with no head. He walked towards it, stopping just at his property line. *Pretty nice job*, he thought. All it needed was a head and some clothes. It had been a long time since he saw a snowman. He knew his neighbor's grandson was visiting but doubted he would be up this early.

After a few minutes of pondering the situation, he decided it warranted no further consideration. He turned and headed back towards his driveway and started shoveling the snow. Several shovels full later, he stopped to wipe his brow. Despite the previous snowfall and cold weather, it was beginning to get warmer, remarkably the snow was already beginning to melt.

SPLAT!—he spun around. This time, he saw a small figure hiding behind the snowman, a little elf of a boy with snow covering the top of his hat, red cheeks, and a mischievous little smile. He heard a giggle, almost musical with a hint of laughter. His laughter rang like tiny bells in the cold air, reminding him of himself as a child.

A smile crossed his own face as he slowly bent down and formed a snowball, stood up, and threw it towards the little figure. He missed his target by only a few inches. He heard another giggle as the figure ran towards him, snowball in hand, ready to be thrown.

SPLAT!—right on target.

"What do you think you're doing, little sir? Don't you know it is dangerous to throw snowballs at people?"

"You threw one at me," another giggle, "and you missed!" They both laughed. It was hard to resist the little fellow. He was so innocent and happy that his laughter was contagious. "My name is Danny. What's yours?

"Hello Danny. I'm Mr. Bachman. Did you make that snowman all by yourself?"

"Yes, but I made it too big and can't reach up to put his head on. Will you help me?" The little boy pleaded with a devilish grin.

"Where are your parents, or your brothers or sisters? Wouldn't you want them to help you?" he asked. Actually, he was hoping there was no one. Helping the little boy with his task wasn't such a bad idea.

"Everyone is still sleeping. So, will you help me? I have the head already made. It just has to be lifted on top."

Without hesitation, Danny grabbed his hand, and they walked over to the snowman's head lying on the ground. His chubby little hands were cold since he wore no gloves, and his little feet in oversized boots made a crunching sound in the snow. The man bent over and picked the head up and placed it on top of the other parts of the body. Judging by its weight, he was surprised the little boy could actually roll such big pieces, and how he got the second one on top of the first was quite an accomplishment for such a little tyke. He admired his hard work and youthful enthusiasm. What had happened to his own enthusiasm for such simple accomplishments?

"Good job. Now all he needs is a hat, carrot nose, and buttons," said Danny. "I'll have to wait till my grandmother wakes up, and I'll ask her if she has a hat and stuff." He stood back to admire his work. "Isn't that the best snowman you every saw?"

Actually, it was, and it was getting hotter and already the snowman had lost a few inches off his girth and a few off his height. By the time his grandmother got up and about, there would be nothing to show of the little boy's hard work. He didn't want the boy to be disappointed.

"You wait here. I think I have just the right stuff for your snowman." He went inside, shaking the snow from his boots. He opened the closet where he stored his old winter things and chose a bright red scarf and an old fishing cap. He went into the kitchen, opened the fridge in search of a carrot. No carrot. But he did find a stalk of celery that would do just fine. On his way out through the garage, he grabbed a pair of worn gardening gloves and headed out towards the snowman.

"Here, I think these will do just fine for our snowman."

It wasn't until he handed the boy the items that he realized he said "our" snowman. He was actually enjoying this. He lifted Danny up so that he could place the hat on the top of the head and wrap the scarf around its neck. Danny couldn't get the celery in place, so he asked him to do it.

"Sure, Danny, but you put these gloves on while I do the nose."

When they were finished, they both stood back, pleased with their work. Again, Danny took his hand and gave it a little squeeze.

"Gee Mr. Bachman, now it looks better than ever!"

His heart felt a little jump as Danny looked up at him with a feeling of pride.

Just then, his neighbor's front door opened.

"Hello Mr. Bachman. I see Danny has found a new friend. Would the two of you like a nice cup of hot cocoa?"

Danny was so excited, he jumped right up, never letting go of his hand and spoke for the two of them.

"Yes Grandma, make it extra chocolaty. Mr. Bachman loves chocolate."

How did he know I liked my cocoa extra chocolaty? he thought with a smile.

Danny's grandmother brought them some chocolate along with several buttons to be placed on the snowman. Danny's mother brought out an old pair of sunglasses.

"It's getting so sunny out that perhaps your snowman could use these!" She lifted him up, and he placed them on top of the celery nose.

"It's time for me to finish shoveling my drive. Thanks for the chocolate." He looked at Danny and asked, "What are you going to call your snowman?"

"I'm going to call him Mr. Bachman, after you." They both smiled.

He picked up the shovel and took one shovel full of snow off the drive and stopped. He took the shovel and placed it back in the garage, went inside and removed his winter things just in time to hear the phone ringing.

"Hello?"

"Sir, I just wanted you to know that the plows are about to enter your street. Your drive should be plowed in a few minutes."

"Don't worry about it. I don't think I'll be going out anymore today." Then he hung up the phone. He walked over to the window and looked at the snowman, now half its original size. It didn't really matter if it melted down to nothing, he thought; next snowstorm, he and Danny would make a bigger and better one.

Then he thought, *I suppose once they clear my driveway I should go out and buy some carrots!*

7
ALIEN ADVENTURES, TRAVEL SERVICE

He sat at the poker slot machine, placing his hand in his pocket and pulling out his last quarter. He had certainly slid to the bottom from playing $1,000 a pot to quarter slots. Gambling started out as a lark, and luck was with him for some time. Then, Lady Luck found another sucker, and he was left with no job, no home, no family, and no self-esteem. Gambling was like a cancer taking over your entire body, the devil taking over your soul, and loneliness taking over your life. His life was now worth a total of only 25 cents.

Before putting the quarter in the machine, he looked around. Even though he was dirty, wearing clothes he must have found in the Salvation Army clothing bin, no one seemed to notice him. Everyone was busy trying their luck at the gaming tables and slots. He was one of them once; how his life had changed. He wondered what time it was. He absently looked at his wrist, no watch. He pawned his diamond watch in for a mere 30 bucks just to have one last play at the tables. What a fool! If he stayed long enough, perhaps the waitress would come around and offer him a drink. He would take coffee with plenty of milk and sugar. He hadn't eaten since yesterday morning. Coffee would do him more good than a 7&7.

Slowly, he lifted his arm, placing the quarter in the slot. He pulled the lever, and one by one, the rollers spun around, showing he had lost. He didn't immediately leave the machine. Instead, he sat wondering what he was going to do next. He had no one to call, nothing else left to pawn, and more of an immediate concern was he had no place to sleep for the night— *Not for the first time*, he thought.

He headed for the bathroom. He was glad no one else was there. He headed for the last stall, his stall, entered, and sat. Had he done this before? He leaned forward with his elbows on his knees, hands under his chin and closed his eyes. Soon, he fell asleep.

How much time had passed, he did not know. There was a loud noise, and he felt something touch his foot. He opened his eyes with a start and looked down and saw nothing but the holes in his shoes. He drifted back to sleep.

Sometime later, he heard activity and realized it was time to leave; where to, he did not know, but he had to make a move. As he moved his feet, he stepped on something. He looked down and saw a leather wallet that probably cost more than his former BMW! He leaned over, hitting his head hard on the stall door. Dazed for what seemed like only a moment, he picked up the wallet. There was something sticky on it, something red. He looked inside. He almost fell into the toilet as he mentally counted out several thousand dollars, credit cards, and a hotel room key. There were pictures of a woman and two children around the ages of five and three. The woman was plain in appearance but had a wonderful, happy smile. The children had the same smile and sparkle in their eyes as though they knew this picture would be something special. Although the picture was your typical K-Mart family photo, there was something strange about it. Then he looked at the driver's license. Mr. Ron Crofton. To his surprise, this Mr. Crofton looked much like himself, except Mr. Crofton was clean shaven, and his own face-was much in need of a shave. The only other thing in the wallet was a business card: "**Alien Adventures**," it said, "the ultimate travel experience."

He slowly left the bathroom and went to the gift shop, where he purchased some toiletries, a jogging suit and pair of sneakers. He decided to see if the key to the hotel room was still valid. It was. He walked into the room and decided the first order of business was to take a shower and shave.

When he was finished washing and put on clean clothes, he looked into the mirror and found that without the beard, he looked exactly like Mr. Crofton. He looked around the hotel room, walked over to the closet and opened the door. His eyes widened. He couldn't believe all the clothes.

Why, this guy must be staying here for months, he thought. Looking over the clothes he noticed all were made of the same material, not necessarily the same style and color, but the same texture. What was it? Not silk, not wool, not a synthetic. He took one of the jackets off the hanger and tried it on. A perfect fit. He bent down and tried on a pair of shoes, again a perfect fit. He felt like Goldilocks visiting the home of the three bears. His stomach grumbled. He had forgotten he hadn't eaten since yesterday. *No,* he thought, *it must be longer than that.*

He walked over to the bed, sat down, and dialed room service. He ordered just about everything on the menu. He was going to enjoy being Mr. Crofton. Thinking it would take some time for the order to arrive, he laid down on the bed and closed his eyes.

There was a loud noise; someone was knocking at the door. Must be room service.

"Mr. Crofton," came a voice outside the door. "Mr. Crofton, it is time to leave." Definitely not room service!

"Who is it?" he asked.

"The limo is here to take you back. There is not much time. Mr. Crofton, open the door."

"Coming." He quickly grabbed the wallet, put it in his pocket, and opened the door. Whoever it was standing there didn't seem to realize he was not the real Mr. Crofton. As a matter of fact, he didn't notice any expression whatsoever. "Just let me get my things, and I will be with you in a moment?'

"There is no time for that and besides, you will have no use for any of these items once you return home."

"Where are we going?"

At this point, the man turned and stood up straight to achieve his full height of about 6'4", towering over him. His face showed anger, but his voice revealed nothing.

"Mr. Crofton, your Adventure is over. You cannot take anything more with you than you came with. Come along, you know the rules. Your family is waiting for you at home."

Fooling this man may have been easy, but how was he going to fool his "family" once he was home. And where was home? It had to be better than living in the street. The man let him pass through the door, then he followed him outside of the hotel where he opened the door to the limo and allowed him to enter. Then he went around to the driver's side, entered and drove away without another word.

It seemed like hours before they left the highway, making their way onto a small, dirt road barely wide enough for the limo to maneuver around the winding pathway. He was getting nervous, yet he was excited.

"Are we almost there?" he asked the driver.

"Surely you know where you are, Mr. Crofton. I think your Adventure here has caused your mind to forget things."

What an idea, he thought with a smile. *I could always claim amnesia!*

At that moment, the road became very bumpy although there didn't seem to be rocks on the road, rather a soft, mud-like consistency. He was sitting far back from the driver now, further than he remembered when first getting into the limo.

A fog seemed to spread throughout its interior, so that he could no longer see the driver. His body seemed to lift and turn, as the car seemed to go up a hill giving a sensation of weightlessness. The fog began to clear. The driver was no longer present. He looked out the window. There was nothing but blackness. He tried to look down, and as he did, a look of horror spread across his face. Far into the distance, he could see the planet Earth getting smaller and smaller until no longer visible.

Mr. Crofton's Adventure may be over, but his was just beginning.

8
A MOST UNUSUAL SUSPECT

Jim Gorman was spread out at the bottom of the stairs, face down, dead! Inspector Reynolds stood next to the body, giving it his complete attention. The usual suspects were all gathered in the living room being questioned by Officer Noland. Inspector Reynolds walked to the doorway and motioned Officer Noland over.

"What have you gotten so far?"

"Well, sir," he answered as he thumbed through his notes. "We have Mrs. Gorman. She just found out her husband was having an affair, so at the moment, she could care less about her husband's present condition. But the gardener verifies her whereabouts. She was at the landscaper with him at time of death."

Inspector Reynolds looked at Mrs. Gorman as she talked to the person next to her. Officer Noland was right; she didn't seem the least bit concerned about her husband's death. Going to pick out plants after you found out your husband was having an affair didn't seem quite right to him.

"What else ya got?"

"Mr. Borgowsky, the family accountant, was here on business. Seems the vic was in debt up to his eyeballs, and Borgowsky found out he was taking money from his various investments. There is no record of whatever happened to the money. That's him next to Ms. Gorman."

Inspector Reynolds noticed that the accountant was a bit fidgety and sitting a bit too close to the deceased wife—much too close. He was sweating. He didn't seem like a man Inspector Reynolds would want to be handling HIS money.

"The woman standing in the back, by the window, is said to be Mr. Gorman's lover. Apparently, she works with the gardener and spends a lot of time here, both in the garden and in the bedroom, but it wasn't until today that Mrs. Gorman found them together. Her name is Theresa Rivers. You might want to question her yourself, sir."

"Why do you say that?"

"She doesn't seem the type to be a mistress. The little house with a white picket fence seems more her style."

Inspector Reynolds took a moment to study Ms. Rivers. She stood looking out the window somewhat in a daze, lost in thought with a worried expression on her face. Officer Noland was correct; she seemed more like the girl next door type. Three suspects but nothing concrete to connect them to the dead body lying on the floor.

"Who's the boy?" he asked.

"That's the mistress's son, Kevin. According to the gardener, the boy spends most of the time with him on the grounds. Mr. Gorman didn't like him spending so much time with the boy. I only talked to him a few minutes. He's a nice kid, too young to really know what is going on. Seems a little slow to me. Gardener says he has some medical problems but said he never really knew what was wrong."

Inspector Reynolds studied the boy at length. He guessed the boy to be around five. He was jingling something in his pockets, and he agreed with Officer Noland that the boy was in a world of his own.

"What proof do we have that Ms. Rivers was, in fact, the deceased's mistress?"

Officer Noland fumbled through his notes again.

"She was in the garden when the vic joined her by the back patio. Ms. Gorman was filling the bird feeder when she saw them in an embrace. Rivers was crying. When Ms. Gorman screamed, she ran away. The gardener said he heard the two of them yelling, and Ms. Gorman told him to take his little bastard and get out. That's when she ran into the gardener, and they went off to the landscaper."

Inspector Reynolds asked Officer Noland to take the wife into the library, where he could question her privately. Ms. Gorman entered the library and took a seat facing Inspector Reynolds but kept her head down.

"Your gardener confirms your alibi for the time of your husband's death, so I'm sure you know that clears you of any charge of murder." She remained silent. "The gardener also says he heard the two of you arguing. What was that all about?"

"I don't see what that has to do with anything."

"Let me be the judge of that, Ms. Gorman. Just answer the question."

Reluctantly, she raised her head and looked squarely into his face. "Do you know what it is like to find out that all your money is gone, and you don't know where or why? Do you know how I felt when I found my husband with another woman? Not only with another woman, but with a woman who is the mother of his child? A child I never knew existed? Yes, we argued. I'm glad he's dead. He made a fool out of me. Whoever did it has my thanks."

Although he found her speech touching, he couldn't resist asking, "Are you having an affair with your accountant, Mr. Borgowski?"

She placed her hands on the desk as she stood and smiled. "So what if I am? Does it really matter now?"

"Yes, Ms. Gorman, it does matter because now Mr. Borgowski is my #1 suspect!"

He then questioned Ms. Rivers.

"Okay now, let's not beat around the bush. We know you had a child with Mr. Gorman. I'm assuming it's little Kevin. I also assume the missing money from the Gorman's accounts has gone for medical treatment for him. What I don't know is if he was giving you the money willingly or if you were blackmailing him."

She stood up quickly, rage on her otherwise calm face.

"I never blackmailed him. He guessed Kevin was his and agreed to pay the medical bills as long as I never told Kevin he was his father or tell his wife. He said he loved his wife, and the child would only bring them further apart."

"What about the scene in the garden?"

"I told him Kevin needed an operation, and I needed more money. He said he didn't have it; that all his funds were tied up or gone. I started to cry, and he tried to calm me down. That's when his wife walked in and started screaming. I left to get Kevin and get out of there before he heard anything."

"Where was Kevin when you found him?"

"He was behind the bench in the garden playing with his marbles."

"Did Kevin like Mr. Gorman?"

She hesitated before replying.

"No, not really. He seemed to become agitated whenever Jim came in the garden. He was especially upset whenever he would hear him yelling."

Inspector Reynolds quickly left the library and went over to the body. He looked on the stairs and called to Officer Noland and asked, "Has anyone moved the body?"

"No," he replied.

"I want you to turn the body over, slowly."

Officer Noland bent down and slowly turned the body over.

Just as Inspector Reynolds suspected. On the steps and under Gorman's body were several clear glass marbles with green and white center swirls. He looked over at Kevin, still sitting in the living room with his hands in his pockets, only now, he had a sinister grin on his face with a coldness in his eyes not there before. Inspector Reynolds walked over to him and put out his hand. The boy slowly took his hands out of his pockets and placed six green and white glass marbles in the palm of Inspector Reynolds' hands. Inspector Reynolds realized then that this little child knew more that was going on than anyone gave him credit for. Inspector Reynolds knelt down and took hold of Kevin's tiny hands and asked, "Kevin, did you put the marbles on the steps so that Mr. Gorman would slip and fall?"

The boy looked over at the body then at Inspector Reynolds with tears forming in his frightened little eyes.

"Yes, sir."

"Why did you do that?"

His reply was simple and to the point: "Because I don't want him to be my daddy." Inspector Reynolds walked over to Officer Noland.

"This case is closed."

9
AND SO IT WAS

"I don't care how you pay for it. I want that fur coat, and I want it in time for the New Year's Eve party at the Sanfords. I don't want to be the laughing-stock of the whole country club by wearing a cloth coat to the party."

"But Estelle, I don't have the money. I had the pool installed, upgraded the kitchen, bought the sports car you wanted, and got you the diamond ring you saw at Tiffany's. You'll have to wait until I can build up some cash."

"WAIT! Listen, Stanley, I have no intention of waiting." She moved closer to him extending herself to her full 6'1" height next to his 5'9". "If I don't get that fur coat in time for the party, then you can just consider the dog house your new home!"

And so it was that Stanley pawned his watch, high school and college rings, his father's gold tie clips, and grandfather's gold pocket watch, and gave Estelle the white, ankle length mink coat that she wanted on New Year's Eve.

On their way to the party, the snow began to fall, and ice formed on the roads. When he made the left turn onto the highway, the car spun around, and the approaching truck hit them head on, killing Stanley instantly with Estelle being taken to the local hospital only to die later on the operating table. But before her death, as she was being transferred to the gurney and brought into the ER, the coveted fur coat fell to the ground almost immediately being covered with snow.

Sally sat in the ER waiting for her little brother to return from getting his hand stitched after cutting it on the sharp edge of a toy. She looked out the window and watched as the woman was rushed through the door and down the hall.

"Sally, Sally, look! I didn't even cry. The nurse gave me a lollypop for being so brave." She looked down at her brother's smiling face. Despite his claim not to have cried, she could see his tear-stained face.

"I'm so proud of you, Chris, now we can go home and watch the ball fall telling us a new year is about to begin. I promise you. Chris, next year will be better for us. I promise."

She took his hand and headed to the walkway that would take them home. They were only five blocks from home but it was cold. As they came to the curb, Chris tripped on the coat that was now covered under several inches of snow. Sally picked him up and in doing so, picked up the coat as well. She wrapped them both in it, and it wasn't until they got home that she realized the beauty but not the value of the item that was keeping them warm.

And so it was that Sally became the owner of a very expensive piece of clothing.

Sally made a pitcher of Kool Aid and popcorn, then sat with Chris to watch the ball fall in Times Square.

"Sally, why didn't Santa come to our house this year?" he asked.

"I think he missed a lot of little children this year. You were a good boy. He will be here next year. Don't worry."

The New Year came and went, and thankfully, spring was just around the corner. The fur coat served them well. They had little money to pay the rent, let alone the heating bill. Both had snuggled under the coat during the cold winter months, but now there were other worries. Chris needed medical treatment, and doctors had done all they could without the needed surgery, for which there was no money. Sally made a decision. She had to sell the coat. So on the first day of spring, she went to the neighborhood pawn shop and sold the coat for enough money for the surgery as well as some money being put aside for Christmas. Thanks to the fur coat, there would be gifts under the tree for little Chris and heat to keep them warm all winter.

Jim was walking past the pawn shop, but turned quickly to get a better look at the white fur coat he saw in the window. It was beautiful but obviously needed a little tender loving care. He thought with a good cleaning, it would make a fantastic gift for his bride to be. Of course, it would have to be shortened. His future bride was only 5'4". As soon as he walked into the shop and touched the coat, he knew he had to have it, regardless of the cost. The smooth pelts were the feel of fine silk.

And so it was; before he knew it, he was heading home with the coat carefully wrapped, held under his arm.

"Oh. Jim! What a lovely gift. Let me try it on."

"Jennifer, you can try it on, but it has to be altered. It is much too long for you."

"You mean it has to be cut. What a shame. it seems like such a waste."

After their wedding Jim and Jennifer went to the furrier, where she was measured once, twice, and three times until the now 3/4 length coat fit her just right. The furrier wrapped up the extra length of coat in a brown bag and Jim took it in one hand while he held the arm of his new bride in the other.

Several months later Jim and Jennifer decided to move from their small apartment into a home of their own and raise a family. They didn't have much to pack and on the day of the final move when the moving van pulled up front, they were so busy that they forgot to check the back hall closet where the brown bag holding the coat remnant lay in the far corner on the floor.

And so it was, that the package was later found by Anna's mother when she moved into the apartment with her daughter and granddaughter, Rebecca.

"Mommy, which room is mine? I want the one at the back of the house, the one with the shelf going all around the room. I can put all my teddy bears up there, and they won't be a mess all over my floor. Please, can I have that one?"

"Rebecca, I thought that room would be Nana's but if it is okay with her, then you can have it."

Nana was so glad just to be living with her daughter that any room would do. She started to place her belongings in the dresser and then opened the closet placing her empty suitcase inside. When she met resistance, she looked down and saw the brown bag, picked it up, and opened it. To her surprise, she found the cutting from the white fur coat.

I know just what I am going to do with this, she thought, and placed it back in the bag and continued to unpack.

For the next three months, Nana spent much of her spare time in her bedroom patiently working on her surprise birthday present for Rebecca. Her arthritic hands caressed the fur and stroked it as she created the treasure worthy of a princess. When it was finally finished, she placed it in a box and wrapped it in sparkling pink paper with a purple and pink bow.

The party was over. Presents were unwrapped, candles blown out and games were played. When everyone had gone, Nana took Rebecca aside and handed her the gaily wrapped package.

Rebecca carefully opened her gift and removed the tissue from inside the box. There she found a beautiful, hand-made teddy bear made of white fur with a nose sewn in with black silk thread and eyes out of buttons from Rebecca's late father's military uniform.

And so it was, that a coat originally obtained by greed, was now a teddy bear being held by a little girl who would love it and cherish it because her Nana had put love in its making and joy in her heart.

10
AND THE NUMBERS ARE...

Prompt: What happens when someone wins lots of money? How does it change their lives?

Rosita sat in front of the TV, waiting for the numbers to be called.

"And the first ball up, and the second, the next, and the next and the last..."

"Rosita, why don't you go out and be with your friends? You should not keep yourself huddled in front of the TV. Go out and have some fun. People like you and me don't win anything. What would you do with all that money if you did win?"

"Oh, Mama, first I would buy you a beautiful house, and you could quit your job. Then I would buy me one of those pretty dresses those women you work for wear. I would have to give the church lots of money since God is the one who told me the right numbers to play in my dream."

"My baby, what numbers? You have been playing them for weeks now and not one has come up. God must have made a mistake."

"God never makes mistakes. Good things come to those who wait, and I am very patient."

Rosita got up, kissed her mother, and off to work she went. She loved going to work in the food kitchen where she helped to prepare hundreds of meals for those less fortunate. She had a smile for everyone and knew everyone by name. She never hesitated to comfort and spread laughter to those who showed up each day for a hot meal. Yes, she had a few favorites and was always able to prepare a little extra for them to take home. This was strictly against the rules, but she didn't care. An apple or biscuit would not be missed.

On her way home, she stopped to buy her lottery ticket with the numbers she claimed God gave her in a dream. Then she stopped by the grocery and picked something for her family to eat for dinner. She had little money, but there was always enough for one or two pieces of candy for her two little brothers. Life was good. She was happy to be alive. She wanted nothing for herself.

"Mama, I'm home. We have good things for dinner. Come see!"

Her mother came into the kitchen and gave Rosita a hug.

"What good things did you bring? The boys are hungry!"

"We have chicken and fresh vegetables. I'll have it ready soon. Put on the TV, so I can hear my numbers called."

Her mother just smiled and left the kitchen, mumbling about the dreams of youth.

"Numbers! Such a silly notion. You should be dreaming of finding a husband instead of dreaming of numbers."

"And if I did find a husband, who would take care of you and the boys?"

Her mother quickly replied: "The same God that speaks to you in dreams would take care of us."

Both women laughed as her mother put on the TV.

What happened next would change their lives forever. At first, it didn't register. They both stood there with their mouths open, hearts stopped. They must have heard wrong. Then they screamed, jumped up and down, and held each other close. It was true! In a dream, God had given Rosita the numbers for the $10 million lottery!

In the following months, the realization of winning all that money sunk in. Of course, Uncle Sam got his share, but there was plenty left for Rosita to do all the things she promised her mother she would do. She purchased a small but lovely home just outside of town for her mother and brothers. It was close to school and the food kitchen. She didn't need a mansion. She needn't impress anyone. She never expected to have so many people, literally come out of the woodwork, asking for money. At first, she gave to many charities, funds, and health care organizations, as well as responded to hundreds of letters expressing their pleas for money. She chose carefully, wanting to make sure they were worthy of any donation she gave.

Rosita eventually became so engrossed in her "new" life that she stopped going to the food kitchen, and she spent less time with her mama and brothers. She went to parties with people who never before even said hello to her. She spent money on frivolous things. Bit by bit, dollar by dollar, she became someone else. Someone she didn't even know.

She came home late one night to find her mother still up.

"There is no need for you to be up, Mama. I'm a big girl now and do not need to have you waiting up for me," she said with a bit of annoyance.

"Don't flatter yourself, my child. I couldn't sleep, that is all." She reached into her apron pocket and pulled out a pink envelope and handed it to her daughter. "This letter is addressed to you."

Rosita didn't recognize the envelope but took it from her mama's hand and walked up the long staircase to her room and closed the door. As she tossed off her $400 pair of shoes, she opened the envelope, expecting it to be another request for money. The words were simple, done with a feeble hand, barely readable. The letter was unsigned. She began to read:

What happened to the girl who once held my hand to comfort a broken heart? You brought me hope though there was none. Your strength brought me courage when I needed to be strong. Your love was an inspiration to many. Although my hands now shake and my eyes are dull, I still remember the child you were. Has all your money brought you happiness or love? Can it bring you riches of the heart? Money used without thought of others will only bring regret. It is what you do with money that brings you happiness. Do you like the person you have become?

Rosita sat for a moment with tears falling down her cheek. She then folded the letter, placing it back inside the envelope and put it in her drawer.

The following day, she returned to the food kitchen she had found such pleasure in many months ago. To her surprise, the walls seemed dirtier, the room darker. There were more people than ever before with less food to feed them. The pots were empty. The laughter she once heard as she walked past was no longer heard. Few people seemed to recognize her as she left the building.

She knew what she would do. It was so simple; why hadn't she thought of it before?

The following night, she sat in silence with her mother until her mother asked, "Rosita, did you hear the good news? Someone donated lots and lots of money to the soup kitchen. You should go down there, they miss you."

"No, Mama, not now. I am sure they have done very well without me. What are you doing tonight?"

Her mother sat at her desk and opened a drawer and pulled out some paper and an envelope.

"Oh, I must bake a cake for a sick neighbor, and I must write some letters to friends to cheer them up. What is my little girl doing tonight?"

Before she answered, she walked over to her mother and bent down to kiss her goodnight. As she did, she noticed the paper sitting on her mother's desk was the same pink paper her anonymous letter writer used. She said not a word. She kissed her and smiled at her, and as she did, she noticed a tear in her mother's eye.

"Thank you, Mama, I am finally happy for the first time in a long time. I love you."

11
A TIME TO REMEMBER

She heard the chimes ringing from a distance. She never realized how clearly they sounded so late at night. It was midnight, and she still hadn't fallen asleep despite the glass of wine she had earlier in the evening.

It was not quite winter yet, and even having several blankets on top of her, she was cold. She had made a fire, putting on the last log he had placed in the rack. Perhaps a cup of tea would help her sleep and warm her up. She reached out to his side of the bed. Not home yet. He seemed to be working later and later every night. She left the bed with what little warmth it offered and slipped into his old leather slippers and put on his oversized bathrobe. Oh, how she loved the smell of him lingering on the fabric. She tied it and flip-flopped down the hall into the kitchen.

She poured just enough water into the kettle for one cup and turned on the stove. Raspberry tea was her choice for the night. She placed the bag into her favorite cup and waited for the water to boil. It didn't take long. She poured the water, waited the required two minutes to brew a good cup of tea, and walked over to the front window and opened the drapes. It was just starting to snow.

She hoped he would be home before the roads were too slippery to safely travel. She looked over toward the antique table with the long-stemmed red rose set in a crystal vase. Wilted now after so many days, but she could not get herself to throw it out. He had given it to her for her birthday, and no matter how much money he might spend on the occasion, the rose was her favorite and most cherished gift.

Now looking out the window, she had to admit that, actually, the snow was quite beautiful, glistening in the streetlight as it descended from the sky, silently landing on the ground. She remembered when she first met him. She had almost forgotten. It was snowing then, too. She was in her parents' driveway, and he was shoveling the adjacent drive for a woman who lived by herself and was too elderly to shovel on her own. How thoughtful he was. He was always that way, and it was one of the main reasons she fell in love with him. Even with snow covering his fuzzy hat and freezing to his mustache, he was able to give her a smile; a smile she would remember forever. The memory of it made her smile now. No words in the dictionary could describe how the memory of that smile made her feel.

She took another sip of her tea as she watched the snow accumulate, lightly covering the street and naked tree branches. She looked at the clock: 1:00. She was getting sleepy. The tea had done its job. She placed the cup on the counter and went back to bed. Again, she reached out to his side of the bed. He won't be coming home. She buried him two weeks ago.

She thought, *I wonder if the snow continues, will anyone be kind enough to shovel my driveway?*

12
FROZEN SNOWMAN

They moved to Alaska when the Alaskan Pipeline was started. He needed work, and she needed a change. They had no family to keep them in Boston, so it was easy for them to pack up and leave. They were in love, and the idea of cold winters with long, sunless nights didn't seem to bother them. The only place they could find to live was 12 miles outside of town, tucked away in a little glen surrounded by fir trees. The only sign of life around them was the train line off in the distance. They made friends of families that had moved there to work on the pipeline, and life was good.

Things started to change, however, when the pipeline was completed, and there was no work to be found. To be more precise, she changed. Having him home 24/7 caused friction between them. She stayed out longer each day and, at times, didn't come home at all.

Winter was here again; the first snowfall was in full swing with about 16 inches of snow already on the ground and at least 18 more inches expected. He put on his warmer clothes and boots to go outside and bring in the chairs and equipment and put them in the shed. It was going to be a long and harsh winter.

As he started to clear away a path in the snow, the wind started to howl causing snow to fall from the tree branches landing on his head and shoulders. He smiled remembering when they first realized they were in love. They were making a snowman, and after they finished putting a carrot in for its nose, they kissed. They knew then that they were made for each other. He put the shovel aside and began to make a snowman. It had to be very large he thought, at least six feet high. He took his time. He wanted it to be just right. It took him almost the entire day to get it ready for her.

When he was finished, he went inside for a hot cup of coffee. It was getting late. He had thought for a long time that she was having an affair, but he didn't want to believe it. Several days and four feet of snow later, she still hadn't come through the door. He looked out the window at the snowman she would never see.

A month later, he called a friend back in Boston who offered him a job. He would go there and start over. He packed up his few belongings, left hers, and drove to the station and boarded the train.

Shortly after leaving the station, he looked over to the glen where his house stood. He could see the snowman in the yard, still dressed up. It would be several months before it was warm enough for the snowman to melt. Several months before anyone would find the body of his wife now frozen inside.

13
CRIES OF TERROR

It was a quaint, picture-perfect town in Maine with a population of 1,200 increasing in summer to about 1,500 once the "wanabees" showed up. We called them "wanabees" because they wanted to enjoy the benefits of small town living until they got bored and the weather turned cold, then they wanted to be back to the hustle of the big city. Sure, we tolerated them because of their money; they had plenty of it, and for the most part, they were a good bunch of people. They enjoyed eating the home cooked meals served at Jane's Juicy Ribs Restaurant and at Keith's Fresh Fish Kitchen, known for its delicious coffee, fresh baked pies, and friendly conversation. You could walk to the town square and have a delicious meal, go up the hill to the one and only movie house showing old movies, then go over to the sweet shop for some ice cream all for under $20. Can't beat that! There was no need to concern yourself about being mugged or afraid to walk alone…until HE came to town. No, you didn't have to worry about anything before then. When HE came, everything changed.

It was the last week in May when the first group of wanabees was due to arrive, so the town was hustling to get ready for the onslaught of visitors that would gradually take over the town for the next three-and-a-half months. As much as the residents complained about their arrival, deep down, they looked forward to the increase in business and meeting the people and listening to the stories about what was going on in the "big" cities. Many of the visitors came back every year, so much so that they eventually became almost like family.

Keith had a little diner that served the best cod sandwiches anywhere in Maine. Today, he had a "WELCOME BACK" sign in the window with a listing of several ways he was going to serve the cod along with a special price for opening day. He was proud of his business, and everyone had to agree he had the best seafood in town.

Jane's restaurant served just about anything you could imagine. This was surprising since Jane never went to culinary school, and the restaurant only fit about 20 people at one time. The tables were covered with white linen then covered with quarter-inch plastic with a mason jar holding silk flowers that had long since lost their shine. She also served the best fresh fruit pies in the state. No kidding—she won blue ribbons for her pies at the State Fair seven years in a row!

The only hotel, "Happy Dreams Lodge," was ready for the first group. The rooms were of average size, and they served a free breakfast of fresh muffins and coffee every morning as long as you were up before 7:00 a.m. Needless to say, not many muffins were served unless there was a group of fishermen going out on an early boat ride.

Town folk waited alongside the depot to check out the new wanabees since it was always fun to welcome people back and see the new guests arrive. That was when they got a glimpse of HIM. A chill filled the air as soon as HE set foot on land. A hush came over the crowd as the visitors walked, as if in slow motion, up the hill to the town square. But HE just stood on the landing, looking around. At first, HE seemed to be looking for someone, expecting someone to be meeting him. When no one came, HE simply bent down to pick up his small, worn valise and smiled. His smile could have made the Devil cry. People backed up allowing him to pass.

———————————————

Over the next week, visitors continued to arrive and take their places at the hotel or rental homes throughout the town, and those that had summer homes took residence for yet another season. It was at Bob's Bakery where everyone seemed to congregate each morning to try out the daily breakfast selection of muffins, bagels, and rolls. This was also the place where people caught up on gossip, stories and, of course, the expectation of who this new man was and what was HE doing in their little town? No one knew where HE was staying, and they hadn't seen HIM since HE first arrived.

"I bet HE's here to open up one of those fancy Walmarts."

"Don't be silly. There aren't enough people here even in peak season to make a big company like that spend all their money and time building a store here."

"Wouldn't it be nice if HE's here to build a Motel 6 or something? We sure could use another hotel," said another.

"I hear HE's here to check out the old Research Station."

Silence filled the room.

Finally, someone spoke.

"Don't tell me you really believe all those stories? Creatures from outer space? Why, I don't believe a word of it."

Bob walked in from the kitchen and poured everyone another cup of coffee.

"I haven't lived here long, but I admit I've heard some strange sounds late at night during a storm. It's not thunder or anything like that. No, if I listen real careful, it's almost like something is talking to me."

One of the customers laughed.

"Oh, come on, Bob, 'something' talking to you? You mean an alien?"

As everyone burst into laughter, the door to Bob's Bakery opened up, and HE walked in. It was almost as though winter brought its brisk weather into the room. Laughter stopped. The man pulled up a chair and sat down. HE picked up the menu then looked up and asked, "Don't tell me you don't believe there are aliens?"

_____

Word spread quickly about the man from outer space. It was almost a week before anyone saw HIM again. HE went over to Jane's, intending to ask her a few questions using the fear HE had already invented to scare her into giving him the right answers, but HE was wrong. She wasn't as sweet as she looked. As soon as the customers saw HIM, they put money on the table and left. The coldness HE brought with HIM seemed to scare everyone except Jane. She looked up at HIM with a sarcastic smile as she said, "You're not very good for business."

"Well, not everyone wants to be in the company of a green creature from outer space."

She laughed.

"That's a joke. You're no more from outer space than you are green. The only green creatures I'll admit to seeing are the little leprechauns I see in my garden. And you sure as hell don't look like any of them."

"You're the first person in this town I've met with a sense of humor."

"Well, I'm not exactly laughing now that all my customers left, so the least you can do is order something."

"Just a coffee and some information."

"The coffee is a buck, but the information may cost you a little more."

HE reached into his inside pocket and pulled out an old photo. As HE did, the smell of death seemed to fall onto the table and to the floor. At first, her eyes burned as she looked at the picture, but as the burning stopped, the picture cleared.

"I'm looking for this man. Have you seen him around?"

"Sure, he's been here. Name's Winston. He rented a shack from old man Jenkins about three months ago. Said he was going to do some hunting. Bought lots of ammunition from the general store. Jenkins tried to tell him there wasn't much more than jackrabbits around here, maybe some deer. All he said was that's not the kind of hunting he intended to do. Come to think of it, he kinda looked like you, not his features or anything like that, but your coldness and that stare you have when you look at people. Like you're looking at me now. Is he a relative of yours?"

"No, no relative."

"Then what you want to find him for?"

"Not that it's any of your business, but I intend to kill the son of a bitch. Thanks for the information."

What the government doesn't want people to know is that their experimentation didn't stop with the use of mice. HE was the result of the most incredible experiment of them all.

Jane went right over to the police station and told the sheriff exactly what was said in her store, word for word. The sheriff listened without saying anything until he was sure she was completely finished with her tale of leprechauns and aliens.

"Jane, have you been puttin' a little somethin' in your coffee? It's not like you to come in here with such a cockamamie story. I admit HE's a little weird. I even think the story about HIM being an alien is more believable than HIM going out in the woods to kill a man. Think about it, HE's been here almost two weeks. Why did HE wait so long to start looking for this guy? I checked with the manager at the Happy Dreams Lodge, and HE never registered there, so where's HE been staying? No rental or lease papers came over my desk. So unless HE's been sleeping with you…"

"Don't be ridiculous!" Jane's face turned *50 Shades of Red*, and for a moment, she was at a loss for words—but not for long. "Listen, Sheriff, you might not want to take this seriously, but don't say I never warned you!"

With that, she turned and stormed out of his office, intending to tell the entire town how she had been insulted by the sheriff and how he refused to follow up and do his job.

The captain wasn't that complacent. He sensed something was wrong with that man from the moment HE appeared in town. He made a few phone calls, and when his deputies showed up, they headed out to old man Jenkins' cabin about 40 miles out of town.

HE knew HE was beginning to change. HE couldn't stop it. HE knew from the past that the look on HIS face would be one of sadness. The type of sadness that comes from knowing what horrific thing was going to happen, yet there was nothing you could do about it. Like watching a child walk along the train tracks and seeing him be hit by a locomotive, sending parts of his body in different directions and seeing that happen over and over again for the rest of your life yet knowing there was nothing you could do to save him.

The bones in HIS face and hands were the first to change. HE could hear their breaking and shifting, gradually becoming so horrific that HE couldn't imagine what HE must look like. HIS skin was now a greenish brown, which meant it was time to discard HIS clothing, so HE would better blend into the woods surrounding HIM. Within moments, HIS clothes would disintegrate, leaving nothing for the dogs to gain a scent. The dogs, they would surely come. HE would have to kill them for sure. A moment of regret touched HIS heart before the final changes took place. Once HIS body changed, the last to diminish, leaving nothing of the man HE once had been, was HIS mind. Now HE was the creature HE was bred to be: A creature with a purpose, with no feelings, with the strength of

100 men, the cunning of a pack of wolves, and the determination of a man with nothing to live for.

Winston was making himself a cup of coffee when he first heard the dogs. He knew what that meant. He knew that HE was close by. He also knew that no matter how much gun power he had, he would not survive the night. It was his fault, all of it. He deserved to die, but not this way.

"Had I made a terrible mistake?" he asked himself for the thousandth time. He was a technician when he allegedly put the wrong vial of serum in the container meant to be taken to the clinic for MS trials. The vial contained serum that proved to cause disfigurement and mental changes in the mice. It also caused abnormal growth spurts in the mice with uncontrollable mood swings. The original experiment was to create a mouse that would be able to hunt smaller creatures on farms and in the jungles, but the project was disbanded due to lack of control of the specimens and lack of funding. The tainted contents of the vial were given to 12 candidates suffering from MS. Eleven died almost instantly. HE was the only one who survived. And now, HE was going to kill the man responsible!

The sounds of the dogs were getting closer. Winston actually thought of killing himself, knowing that the death HE had planned would not be a painless or pretty one. He had hoped he would be given a chance to explain what he had found out, that it was a plan all along to further advance their experimentation. If only he could speak to the man before HE changed into the monster HE'd become. They both lost their jobs, families...everything. Wasn't that enough?

No, how could it be.

More barking. The door opened, and there HE was, the most horrible creature he had ever seen. It was too late for talk. Winston squeezed the trigger of his rifle, right on target. Nothing. Another round. Nothing.

"I'm sorry, please forgive me, but I don't think it was an accident."

The creature cocked his head and let out a sound like an animal caught in a bear trap.

Another round. Then two dogs leaped through the door towards the creature. In seconds, they were torn to pieces.

The first dart came through the window, landing in Winston's neck. Before he was down, the second dart hit the creature in his shoulder, crashing him down. Two men walked in wearing DSI uniforms.

"Tell the men to clean this mess up before that bumbling sheriff and his deputies get here," said the man in charge.

The other man looked down at the creature and asked, "What now? Winston is getting too close to the truth. Sooner or later, he's going to tell the world what really goes on at the lab, and maybe the next time, we won't get here in time to control that thing."

"We'll take them back to the lab, and by the time we're through with them, they won't remember a damn thing. A few more corrections in the formula, and all this should be behind us."

"And if we can't adjust the formula?"

"There are always plenty more *volunteers*."

When the sheriff arrived at the cabin, there was no sign of any struggle or evidence of wrong-doing. The populous went about their business, and they never saw HIM again. Talk about aliens gradually stopped. But elsewhere, there were cries of terror that could not be heard!

14

GAS

7:45 a.m. #12 Cranberry Lane

Jane and Tom were finishing breakfast when Jimmy came running down the stairs, throwing his bookbag on the sofa.

"I love this house, I love my new room, and I especially love my new school! Can you believe there is actually a bathroom on every floor, and the cafeteria's awesome! I'm so glad we moved here."

"Well, I'm glad to hear that because it's too late to change our minds now. Sit down and eat your breakfast before it gets cold," his mother said, smiling as she placed his eggs and sausage in front of him.

Jimmy looked at his mother, laughing, and asked, "Did you burn the sausage? I smelled it all the way up into my room."

"I did no such thing! Do those sausages look burned to you?"

"No, but I did smell something upstairs. Must have been my dirty gym clothes. I forgot to put'em in the hamper. I better hurry or miss the bus."

"Your father and I have to go into town this morning. We'll take you to school today." Tom picked up his briefcase, ushered his family out the front door, and locked up.

8:10 a.m. #14 Cranberry Lane

Sally and John had set the alarm for 7:30, but just couldn't manage to get up. Yesterday, they painted the entire downstairs of their new home with two coats of paint in each room. They were more than tired. John reluctantly got out of bed, stretched, then shook Sally trying to get her up.

"Come on honey, we have a lot more painting to do today, no lollygaggin'."

"Do I have to get up?" She literally rolled out of bed, practically falling to the floor, but she caught herself just in time. "God, am I tired. What in the world is that smell?"

"Probably just the smell of the paint. It rained most of the night, so nothing had a chance to dry. Come on, lazy bones, get dressed. We'll drive down to Lowe's and get the rest of the paint. With luck, we should be able to finish the job before dinner."

"You mean if we don't die first."

So, after a quick shower and grabbing a donut from the fridge, they both left the house in search of more paint for the rooms upstairs.

8:30 a.m. # 16 Cranberry Lane

Charlene was usually up much earlier and should have finished her run by now. She felt a little groggy but was determined to do her five-mile run before going about her daily routine. She would be glad when they finished all the construction. The smell must be coming from the asphalt they put down on the lower end of the street yesterday. She was hoping they wouldn't finish building so soon since she liked seeing the open woods and the fact she could sit in the back yard and have her coffee in the morning and dinner at night in some degree of privacy. Oh well, progress is progress. Hopefully she would meet some nice people. So far she met John and Sally. They seemed okay. Perhaps she could get them to join her in a run in the mornings.

She finished lacing up her running shoes and left her house for her brisk morning run.

9:45 a.m. #52 Cranberry Lane

Mary Collins lived alone with her 12-year-old Yorkie named Fluffy. She would be glad when the other houses were completed on her block. She was the first one to be built but the last lot on the curve of Cranberry Lane, and she felt isolated from the rest of the community, not being visible to the rest of the houses. She was anxious to meet new neighbors. For the most part, she lived a rather regimented life, and today was her cleaning day. She was vacuuming the living room. Although the TV was on, the vacuum drowned out the sound.

Suddenly, she felt a tremendous jolt, and the entire house shook. Fluffy began to bark and shake. Mary continued to vacuum as she went over to Fluffy and patted her head.

"It's okay, don't worry. It's just all that construction going on. Don't be nervous." She didn't hear the bulletin that came over the TV news station about the gas explosion on Cranberry Lane and that evacuation procedures were completed with everyone having been advised to go to their designated shelter. THIS WAS AN EMERGENCY!

Again, the house shook. Fluffy barked, but it was too late. Mary never even heard the next explosion.

15

HEXAKOSIOIHEXEKONTAHEXAPHOBIA*

Meaning: fear of the number 666

She sat in the waiting room. No matter how early she arrived, she was always the sixth person in line even though she was supposed to be the only 6:00 a.m. appointment

Finally, she walked into the dusty, dimly lit room and sat at the small, round table. The scarf that was placed on the table was brightly colored, out of place for such a dark room. The woman sitting opposite her nodded her head briefly, no smile; never looked up to see her face. She placed the cards on the table, mumbled a few words, then picked them up and dealt the cards, face down, in a pattern of six consecutive cards. The tarot cards were once as colorful as the scarf but now faded due to many years of use.

One by one, she turned the cards over, giving an explanation for each one. She turned over the card nearest the young woman, the main card, the card that truly told the story she had come to hear. It was the Lovers card, the number-six card. This represented peace, calm, contentment, self-acceptance, and satisfaction. She then turned over the card adjacent to the Lovers card. This card meant nothing in itself, but due to its position and the card previously shown, meant that the number-six card's meaning was to be reversed.

The woman then took hold of her hand and explained that her life's path described her journey through life and the major lessons she must learn in this lifetime. To determine one's life's path, you must add the numbers of your day, month, and year of birth then do some mathematical mumbo-jumbo that only she seemed to understand and come up with a number. Her life's path or destiny number was number six, which meant that her Lover's card, now reversed, represented the Devil, and she was now a possessor of a captivated spirit.

When her reading was finished, she left the room almost laughing.

"A possessor of a captivated spirit." What the hell was that supposed to mean?

The number six. What's in a number? Why was hers the number six? Let's see, 666 refers to "the Beast," and according to the Book of Revelations, the Beast is believed to refer to the Devil. *Six is associated with many things*, she thought. *The numbers on a roulette table sum to 666. Six represents the six directions (north, east, south, west, up and down.) Man was created on the sixth day, 60 seconds in a minute, 60 minutes in an hour, 6x6 inches in a yard, six major members in the human body, six quarts of blood in man, man is buried six-feet in the ground, and the population right now is 6 billion.*

She thought about all the mathematical and theological and cultural related meanings for the number six. All were just coincidences. But what concerned her were the words of the tarot reader: "You are now a possessor of a captivated spirit."

She went to work as usual, but when she sat down at her CPU computer, she noticed it was a 666 MHZ Pentium III built in 1999. Her desk phone number was 555- 666-6661. More coincidences?

By the time she arrived home, she was starting to get anxious. She was not calm or content and certainly not satisfied. Her life's path was certainly reversed. What does a "captivated

spirit" mean? She looked in the mirror. She looked the same...
or did she? Did she look older? Was her hair greyer? Her hands
were cold, and she began to shake.

The phone rang, startling her. She let it ring. It rang six
times before she picked it up. No one was there. Was there
really a spirit trapped in her body? A spirit wanting to be set
free? How could she set it free? Then she wondered what the
spirit would do once it was set free. Would it be a kindly spirit,
thankful for its release, or would it be a spirit of violence that
would strike a blow causing her own demise?

She climbed into bed, clothes still on, and covered herself
with warm blankets, but still she was cold. She looked at the
clock: 12:06 a.m. ...12 is 2x6 and six—three sixes. She lied still,
thinking, *The corresponding card is the Devil; that is what I am
inside. I am the "possessor of a captivated spirit"...but whose spirit?*

When it was time for her to get up, she ran out and down
the street to the tarot reader. She had to have some answers.
When she got there, she stopped short and looked up at the
address, 666 Devil's Court. Her heart began to pound as she
opened the door and walked in. No one was there; she was the
first one to arrive. She waited, but no one else came in. Slowly,
she got up and walked toward the small room and opened the
curtain. There was no table, no cloth, no gypsy reader, and no
tarot cards.

The cards were right, she realized. *My life's path represented
my journey through life and the meaning of the number-six card was
reversed. My life is moving in reverse. It was my spirit that wanted
to be set free. Now I have a chance to start my life over. If man was
created on the sixth day, then I have six days to recreate my own life.
What shall I be?*

When she left the building, she had a quickness to her step,
a sinister smile on her lips and a cruel, calculating look on her
face. The captivated devil within just came out.

16
IT'S A BARNUM AND BAILEY WORLD

It was Grandpa Mike's birthday, and his family was traveling south to celebrate his ninetieth birthday. Samuel, age eight, and Peter, age 10, were sitting in the back of the car arguing over who gets to use the iPod while their mother, Peg, and father, Matthew, were in the front. Peg was trying to read the map over the commotion in the back seat, and Matthew was concentrating on the icy road ahead.

"Will you two please be quiet?" pleaded their mother. "I'm having enough trouble trying to figure out which way to go without the two of you arguing over a stupid game."

"Ohhhhh! Mom, you said 'stupid'!"

"I'll say more than that if you don't be quiet."

"I think we should all be quiet, so I can concentrate on the road," Matthew interjected. "If I remember correctly, we should only be about 30 miles away. I expect you two to be on your best behavior. Remember, Grandpa is going to be 90, and he doesn't like a lot of noise."

The boys suddenly became very quiet, looked at each other, and began to laugh. Sam was the first to speak.

"Grandpa can't hear very well anyway. All he ever talks about is when he was little, and he's always talking about the circus. I don't even think he remembers when he was a little boy."

"Dad, did Grandpa really run off and join the circus?" Peter asked.

"I doubt very much if he ever 'ran' off, but your grandfather always had some wonderful stories about the circus, and every chance he had, we would sit together, and he'd tell me about when he was young and how hard life in the circus was. 'The Greatest Show on Earth,' he would say, 'America's Living National Treasure.' He would go on and on. I doubt if they are true, but if he wants to tell you the stories, just let him. One day, you'll look back and tell your own children some of those stories. Just humor him and let him enjoy the telling of the story whether it is true or not. It's part of your family heritage."

Sam gave a long sigh as Pete asked, "But if we don't know if all those stores are true or not, then how can they be part of our heritage?"

"That, my son, is up to you to decide."

Dinner was over, and Pat was in the kitchen cleaning up, Matthew was trying to fix the TV remote, and Grandpa was sitting by the fire with the two boys, once again telling stories from memories of long ago.

"Yes, I remember my life in the circus but the circus started long before I came along. It was in 1919 that James Bailey and P.T. Barnum merged and established Ringling Brothers Circus. They first appeared in New York City."

"I was in New York City once," interrupted Samuel. "Remember, Pete, we went to Radio City for the Christmas show? We ate at Applebees, remember?"

"Yes, I remember. Go ahead, Grandpa, tell us more."

"Well, back then, the circus travelled from town to town in small caravans with animal-drawn wagons. It was the largest traveling show of all time. They had JUMBO, the world's largest elephant. Children came from all over just to see him. There was Gargantua, an enormous gorilla, almost as big as the elephant. Scared the daylights out of all the people. But then the depression came, and no one had the money to buy food, let alone go to a circus. But with the help of President Roosevelt giving the circus special dispensation…"

"What's dispensation?"

"President Roosevelt gave the circus special permission to use the railroad to transport all the animals and tents from one city to another. That was in 1942, during the war. With his help, the circus stayed alive. But still, circus life was not easy. One of the worst fires in the United States was in Hartford, Connecticut. About 8,500 people attended the circus when a fire broke out. A tramp clown named Emmett Kelly tried to get the fire out with a bucket of water, but it didn't help much."

Samuel began to laugh, "Oh, Grandpa, how could he put the fire out with only a bucket!"

"Well, he couldn't. That's how come 100 people died that day. The famous actor Charles Nelson Reilly, then 13 years old, survived the fire, and when he got bigger, he wrote a play called *The Life of Reilly*, where he depicted the fire in the play. But it was long after that when I joined the circus in 1968. It was when the Feld brothers and some others established the Ringling Brothers and Barnum & Bailey Clown College. I learned a lot. It wasn't all fun and laughter. It was hard work making people laugh."

Both boys stared at their grandfather in amazement and said in unison, "YOU WERE A CLOWN!"

Their grandfather looked down at the boys and simply said, "Yes, I was always a clown. As a matter of fact, I'm still trying to make people laugh."

At that point, Peg and Matthew walked in and sat on the couch next to the boys.

"That's enough story-telling. It's almost time for bed you guys," their mom said.

"Just a little more time, please," the boys begged.

"There isn't much more to tell," their grandfather stated. "The circus grew, and in 1971, it was sold to Mattel for $40 million. Can you believe that? Many things have changed since then. Only two circus trains remain, each one mile long with 60 cars. Despite what PETA says, the animals of the circus received the best of care. Their health and welfare are the circus's first priority. 'The circus believes that promoting human and animal interaction is vital to increasing public awareness of the need to protect and preserve animal species.' All the dogs are from animal shelters; they have a center for elephant conservation in Florida for breeding and retirement of its Asian elephants and sponsor breeding programs for their endangered species. Some organizations oppose the use of domestic animals in circuses and want animal-free circuses. Can you imagine a circus without an elephant?"

"Okay, boys, that's enough. Time for bed. We head for home early, and we all have to get our sleep."

Several years later after their grandfather had passed, the family went to his home to dispose of his belongings to make way for the new owners. While Peg and Matthew were cleaning out the garage, Pete and Sam, now both in college, found themselves packing boxes and exploring the hidden treasures in the attic.

"Hey, Pete, look at this trunk. It must be 100 years old."

"It's an old traveler's trunk, a steamer's trunk I think it's called. Can you believe it?"

The wood, although old, still had the finish and smell of a finely crafted piece of furniture. The leather strapping was worn and stained from years of use and weather worn. On the front in what was once brightly red and gold letters were the words "The Greatest Show on Earth." Although eager, the boys gently undid the straps and opened the trunk. Smiles filled their faces, and instantly all the stories their grandfather told came racing through their minds. On the top were a red clown nose and a yellow frizzy wig. Under that were several clown costumes obviously worn many times, including the large clown feet, makeup, and all the accessories used by circus clowns. There was a faded folder tucked in the bottom of the trunk tied with a torn ribbon. Pete gently untied the bow placing it on top of the trunk. Inside was a diploma from the Ringling Brothers and Barnum & Bailey Clown College with their grandfather's name printed in gold letters and paper clippings about the great Connecticut fire where 100 people were killed, many never being identified. There were pictures of their grandfather with other circus performers as well as one of him with an offspring of JUMBO the elephant.

The boys called down to their parents, telling them to come up to see the trunk. As their father looked down at all the costumes, pictures, and memorabilia, a tear ran down his cheek.

"I didn't realize all those stories were true."

Peg put her arms around her husband and whispered, "This is the heritage your father wanted to keep alive, so we'll keep his stories alive for him."

"How will I do that?" he asked.

Peg picked up the clown nose and placed it on Matt's nose and said softly, "You'll find a way."

17
IT'S A DEAL

He walked up the block, looking for the address he had been given: #12 Cherry Street. He didn't know how he let his friends talk him into this, but they insisted this would be a good idea. It was a quiet neighborhood with women sitting on their steps, laughing and talking with neighbors. Men were dealing cards on the porch while children played ball in the street.

He walked a little farther before coming to the address he wanted. It was an old brownstone gravely in need of repair. Instead of curtains, there were wrought iron-scrolled security casings on the lower floor. The second-story windows were void of any covering showing the dirt and cracks in the glass. The steps were worn, and he was careful as he approached the front door for fear of falling through the wood. He looked at the card he was holding once again: "Psychic Readings. If You Don't Believe, You Soon Will."

He shook his head thinking twice about what he was about to do but before he had a chance to change his mind the door opened, apparently by itself. He took a deep breath, hesitated, then cautiously walked in and looked around the foyer. Aside from the dim light coming through the soiled windows, the area was dark. There was a glass-top table to the left and to the right stood a coat rack with one well-worn coat hanging from it.

"Mr. Dean James. how nice of you to have come, and on time. I'm impressed."

He turned quickly to see the man who had spoken in such an icy tone.

"Hello, I'm here to see Mr. Romeo."

"Well, you are in luck." He extended his small, well-manicured hand. "I'm Mr. Romero. Please call me Damian. Come into the parlor."

Said the spider to the fly, he thought.

"I know this must all seem strange to you, but I assure you, there is nothing to be wary of. If, for any reason, you wish to discontinue our conversation, feel free to say so, and you are free to leave."

Did he think I thought he was going to tie me up and keep me prisoner? he wondered.

"I assure you, Mr. James, I never thought that at all."

Damian led him into a small room at the back of the house and both took a seat around a table covered in a dark, purple cloth.

"Let's get started, shall we?"

Even if he wanted to leave, he was transformed into a believer as soon as he sat down.

"You came here because you want me to contact your wife. Isn't that correct?"

"Yes, she has been dead for two years."

"Actually, Mr. James, the longer it is that a loved one has entered into the light, the harder it is to communicate. You continue to visit her grave every day. The constant grieving must, at some point, come to an end."

"Perhaps you have never loved anyone as I loved my wife. I want you to let me see her one last time. I never had a chance to tell her how sorry I am. I was told you would be able to help me. If not, I'll be on my way."

Damian remained silent for a moment before taking Dean's hands, placing them flatly on the table before him. He then quietly whispered into the room with some unfamiliar tongue, so Dean could not distinguish the words. As soon as Damian was finished speaking, it became cold with a stale odor filling the room. Perspiration formed on Dean's forehead as his body began to relax and almost float out of his chair.

"A departed soul doesn't always wish to come back into the world of the living," Damian said. "But then there are times when a soul wishes to return. If that happens, an exchange must be made. What would you give me, James, to see your wife one last time?"

"I'd give anything."

"Anything?"

"Yes, I would give anything, even my life."

"Good, then it's a deal. Let us begin."

With that, Damian held Dean's hands tighter as he intoned the unknown words. Frost formed on the windows and along the floor boards. Overhead a hazy, gray film of light swirled, slowly taking shape. Dean watched in disbelief. The image moved closer, and the closer it got, the more identifiable it became. It was his wife, as beautiful as he remembered, if not more so. Her golden hair was longer than he recalled, and her eyes were the color of moonlight on an ocean wave. But as the apparition floated directly before him, her lips were trying to tell him something. He looked closer. She whispered: "GO, go quickly, before it's too late."

He pulled his hands away and stood up, shaking, as he looked at his wife as she slowly vanished into the mist in which she had come. He knelt down, crying, and praying that she would reappear.

Damian stood and walked over to him and put his hands on Dean's shoulder. He leaned down and spoke into his ear, "Now, it is time for me to collect on our deal. Your soul is mine."

Dean started to scream, tears running down his face.

"My soul! What the hell are you talking about? You said I could talk to her; tell her I was sorry. I wasn't able to say a word. She vanished before my eyes, before I could tell her…"

"Before you could tell her what? That you were sorry she is dead and you survived? Sorry that because of you she no longer walks among the living? That you are the reason she is dead? Is that the reason you visit her grave every day? Because you are guilty of murder?"

"I did not murder her. She was at the wrong place at the wrong time. I was the one who should have died that night."

"Ah, but you are dead. I've had your soul as soon as our deal was made. The deal was that I'd let you see your wife. I never said you would be able to talk to her. That was not the deal. You freely offered me your life. Now I'm taking it. She was a good woman. I no longer have use for her soul. You were unfaithful to her, and she took her life as a result. I took her damaged soul just long enough to get you to come to me. Yours is the soul I wanted. I have set hers free."

Several months later, Andrea James casually walked down Cherry Street on her way to the theater and felt a cold chill as she approached #12. She looked at the old brownstone and wondered how anyone could let such a beautiful house deteriorate so. She started to walk up the steps. It was as if someone was calling to her. The door slowly opened, beckoning, inviting her in. Cautiously, she entered the foyer and looked around. She started to shiver. She took several steps before she heard something familiar. Then, all of a sudden, she heard a faint whisper — "GO, go, before it's too late."

18
JUNE BRIDE

Samantha sat on the velvet covered arm chair in the reception area of Christos Boutique on Madison Avenue as she waited for Randy to join her. They were going to pick out favors for their June wedding. He was 40 minutes late.

Samuel was also waiting and absently skimming through the latest edition of *Brides* magazine. His fiancée was going to show him the bridesmaid dress she and her maid of honor chose for their June wedding. She was an hour late.

Monique, the receptionist, picked up the phone on the first ring, listened to the message, then made an announcement: "Will Sam please come to the front desk? There's a message for you."

Both Samantha and Samuel rose from their seat and walked over to the receptionist and simultaneously asked, "You have a message for me?"

The receptionist, a little confused, answered, "I have a message for Sam from a Randy."

Samantha gently pushed Samuel out of the way, "I believe that message is from my fiancé. Where can I take the call?"

Monique was embarrassed as she replied in a whisper, "He is no longer on the phone. He wanted me to tell you that he is not coming and that the wedding is off."

"What? Did he leave a number for me to call him back? What does he mean 'the wedding is off'? It's only five weeks away. How can this be happening?"

Just then the phone rang.

"That must be him calling back, let me speak to him."

The receptionist picked up the phone, listened to the message, then handed the phone over to Samuel. As he listened to what was being said, he began to smile and shake his head. He hung up the phone without a word.

"Well, Monique, looks like I won't be viewing any dresses today or any other day. My fiancée just dumped me." He looked over at Samantha's stricken, tear-stained face and asked, "Want to go for a cup of coffee, or something stronger? I think we could both use one."

"I just don't understand. We've been planning this for three years. He helped me pick out the flowers, reception hall, cake, photographer, limo service. Everything. He wouldn't let me use a wedding planner. He said he wanted us to do it all ourselves. He even took on the responsibility for the music and honeymoon. He said he wanted me to be surprised."

"Well, he certainly did that, didn't he?" His remark was somewhat harsh, but he said it with a grin.

"What do you mean?" She lifted her left hand up to his face letting him get a good look at the ring on her finger. "This is a 3-karat diamond by Ritani. He loved me!"

"At this point, it might as well be a cigar band, and evidently he didn't love you as much as you thought."

"Well, you're not much better off, are you? Oh, God, I almost forgot. I was to pick up my wedding dress this afternoon. What am I going to do? It's all paid for. It's a beautiful Amalia Carrara in pure silk, pale Pink Vodka with a leaf and crystal tiara."

"It seems like you're more upset about not wearing the wedding gown than losing your fiancé."

"I don't like your tone. At least you don't have to pay for a dress that you are not going to wear!"

He smiled, "I don't think I'd look very good in a dress. My knees are too bony. I'm also bow-legged."

His smile made the tears flow once again. She lowered her head and said, "I'll take you up on that drink."

Samantha was on her third gin and tonic when she said, "I just don't understand it. We already had the invitations printed and our silverware and China was all picked out. What in the world made him suddenly decide not to go through with the wedding? It was his family that wanted to make a big deal, having the wedding at the Mansion in Jersey. I just wanted a small, intimate dinner with close friends and family. I admit I did get a little carried away with all the fan fair…"

Sam seemed more relieved than upset about his wedding being cancelled.

"I didn't actually care what Andrea wanted. Whether she chose roses or daisies meant nothing to me, but the further into the wedding plans we got the more I felt we were making a mistake. Actually, this is probably all for the best. When I finally met her mother at the engagement party, she actually gave me her room key, inviting me to her room after dinner. Now that would have been a real problem."

"How can you be so blasé about all this? She probably knew you were having second thoughts and figured she should dump you before you had a chance to dump her. Maybe she found out you went to her mother's room. She's pretty lucky if you ask me."

"No one asked you. And what makes you think I was crazy enough to go to her room? What do you think **you** did to piss **him** off?"

"Me! Why do you think it was my fault?"

"Be honest, what guy wants to spend all his time picking out flowers, furniture, going to taste testings for cake and dessert? He probably felt smothered by it all."

She started to cry.

"But it was his family that wanted all that stuff! I just went along with it."

"It was your wedding, not his family's. Anyway, I'm probably way off base." He was trying to make up for his assumptions and making her feel bad but her tears kept coming.

"Have another drink."

"No, I think I've had enough. I better go home."

When they got up, he noticed she was unsteady on her feet, so he held her arm as they walked from the bar into the restaurant.

"How about we both get something to eat? I could do with a good steak. How about you?" Without waiting for a reply, he waved to the waiter, who directed them to a private table for two in the corner. They ordered steaks, and by the time the order came, she was calmed down and even able to smile at some of his humorous stories about his own wedding plans.

"I guess I did get caught up in all the preparations. Perhaps I did smother him with all his responsibilities."

Now he really felt sorry for what he had said earlier.

"No, he's probably just a jerk."

She looked up and again noticed his smile. Randy may have given her a beautiful ring, but he never gave her such a charming smile. Yes, Sam was right; Randy was a jerk.

They had just finished their meal and ordered an after-dinner drink when Sam looked up and caught his breath. Seating in the far corner was his ex-fiancée, Andrea, sitting mighty close to a man and just about to kiss him on the cheek.

Samantha, after noticing the strange look on Sam's face, turned her head to follow his gaze. If she thought Sam's face looked angry, hers were even angrier. There he was—Randy, kissing another woman. Her voice was louder than she realized when she said, "Well I'll be damned. Can you believe it? It didn't take him long to find some starry-eyed floozy to share **his** bed."

Sam's reply was not what she expected.

"I'll have you know that floozy is my ex-fiancée. Let's go over and say hello."

She protested only slightly as Sam took her hand, pulling her over to the opposite table. Randy and Andrea seemed to be in shock as Sam spoke:

"Randy, I believe you know Samantha. Andrea, I would like you to meet my lover, Samantha. We've been seeing each other for several months now. You both did us a great favor today by breaking off the wedding since we didn't know how to tell you we were in love. It was love at first sight. Wasn't it my dear?" He looked down at Samantha who was unable to speak. He bent down and gave her a kiss better reserved for the bedroom. "Well, it was nice running into you both. Samantha and I must be going. We have lots of planning to do. June is just around the corner."

19
JUST AROUND THE CORNER

Claire was running late. It wasn't easy working 10 hours a day being a single mom with an energetic eight-year-old. Jenny was in the third grade but doing school work at a fifth-grade level. She was a big help to her mom but a child nonetheless.

"Jenny, Mommy can't be late for work. Are you sure Stephanie didn't say anything to you yesterday about her not coming here today?"

Jenny was busy making her own lunch and getting her books ready for school and didn't hear her mother's question. Stephanie, "Stef," had been Jenny's babysitter for the past five years, ever since Claire got her divorce. For the most part, the divorce was an amicable one. No one was at fault; they just grew apart and wanted to go their separate ways.

"Jenny, answer me, did Stephanie say she wasn't coming in today?"

"No, she said nothing to me."

"I have to get going, and the bus will be here any minute. Can you walk to the bus stop yourself just this once? I'm sure Stephanie will be here shortly and will be able to meet you at the bus stop after school. The stop is just around the corner, and I know you know the way. Hurry up, grab your things, and we can leave together." Claire picked up her brief case as she pushed Jenny through the door ahead of her locking the double bolt behind her. "Stephanie has keys to the house; she'll be here shortly. She's probably waiting for you at the bus stop right now. Nothing to worry about. Give mommy a kiss."

Jenny reached up and put her arms around her mom's neck and gave her a kiss and said, "I love you, see you later."

Claire was in too much of a hurry to reply. She knew Jenny could take care of herself. She got in the car, and as she drove away, she looked into the rear-view mirror and could see her daughter skipping around the corner to the bus stop.

Several hours later, Jenny got off the bus and looked around for Stef. Jenny was the only child that used this stop, so there were no other mothers or students around. She proceeded to walk home with her backpack swaying from side to side, carrying the artwork she did in art class that afternoon. It was just a short walk. She would be home in a minute. When she got home and walked up the front steps, she noticed the front door was open.

"Stef, I'm home! Come see what I made in class." She didn't wait for an answer: Stef must be inside, why else would the door be open? Jenny removed her back pack as she went through the door and dropped it on the floor. The first thing she felt was fear, then pain. She landed on the floor just seconds after her backpack.

How much time passed, she didn't know, but when she regained consciousness, she found herself in what she felt was a box, barely large enough to hold her trembling body. Holes had been punched through for air and allowed a small amount of light to shine through.

Still daylight, she thought. Someone had placed a water bottle alongside her, but she was hesitant to drink from it despite the fact she was very thirsty. Who knew what might be inside? She scrunched herself together and maneuvered her legs so that she could brace herself up and peer out one of the holes. She felt a sharp pain in her head. Tears fell from her eyes as she controlled herself not to scream out. She could hear nothing except her heart beating.

Then she heard a door open, and heavy footsteps moved toward her. She assumed it was her attacker. She remained as quiet as possible. He forcibly hit the box several times with a heavy object. She cried out then she fell into darkness. Blood seeped out onto the floor. Then there was silence once again.

Claire headed home. She never worried about not getting home in time for dinner. Stephanie always made sure Jenny did her homework and had a good dinner before she went to bed. Time allowed, she would even take Jenny to the park before dinner. She certainly was a big help.

She pulled the car into the garage and made her way into the kitchen. All was dark. She went over to the phone and saw the message machine blinking. She must have forgotten to check her messages from last night. She turned it on.

"Mrs. Warner, this is Stephanie. I'm so sorry to call so late, but I have a family emergency and won't be able to come over for several days. If you want Annie to fill in for the time being, give her a call. You have her number. Again, I'm sorry for any inconvenience."

Now Claire was starting to worry. The house was open, dark, and Stef never came over today. Where was Jenny? Claire quickly put her things down and rushed through the house calling, "Jennifer?"

After a look in the basement, she ran out back. Nothing. It wasn't until she came back in and went into the hall that she saw Jenny's backpack, and then she saw the blood.

The police responded to the 911 call within minutes. Normally, there is a waiting period for a missing person of 24 hours, but not in the case of an eight-year-old.

"When did you notice she was missing?"

"When I came home from work."

"Do you normally let her go to the bus stop herself?"

"No, I was running late, and I thought Stephanie was going to be at the bus stop."

"When did you realize that your sitter hadn't come in today?"

"I noticed my machine had a message. She had an emergency and couldn't come."

"Has Jenny ever walked to the bus by herself?"

"No, never."

"Then why did you let her go today by herself?"

"I was running late. The stop is just around the corner. I thought she would be okay."

"Could she have run away? Were there any problems at home?"

"No, never! Why would you even think that?"

The questioning continued for hours, not only with her but with every neighbor and anyone that had been in contact with the child. Jenny's father was originally the prime target for investigation since most family abductions are a violation of a custody agreement. He also had access to the home, and there are just as many home abductions as those outside the home. But he was quickly ruled out. Jenny's dad was out of the country at the time of the abduction.

The disappearance of a child requires immediate attention from the entire community, sound data is required. Unfortunately, based on the evidence at hand, Jenny was missing almost seven hours before the police were notified. Seventy-four percent of abduction cases by a violent party result in victims being dead within three hours after the abduction, and generally, children under five are more apt to be found dead.

Approximately 350,000 family abductions (abductions by a family member) occur each year, many resulting in mental harm, physical abuse, and sexual abuse; 58,200 non-family abductions occur each year. The total juvenile missing children cases a year total 801,332, which include family and non-family abductions, runaways, and thrown-aways.

We may never find out what happened to Jenny, but we do **know that whatever happened did not happen "just around the** corner," but in her own home where she should have been safe.

Source of Information: National Center for Missing and Exploited Children, FBI and NCIC

20
LIFE IS FULL OF SURPRISES

Who would have thought when they woke up in the morning, got dressed, and went to work that by the end of the day they would be a murderer?

That's just what happened to James Woods on a cold February morning. He did his usual morning schedule, same old stuff, and headed out to his garage to warm up his car. The weather was bitter with frost on the roof of the car despite it being garaged. He sipped his coffee while he waited for the inside of the car to warm up enough so that he could no longer see the white mist of air when he exhaled. Ready to go. He backed out the driveway and headed north toward Cleveland Street. It was early, 4:45 a.m. He was lucky he lived not too far from work. He hated his job, but the fact he didn't have to drive too far, considering the price of gasoline, made it a little more tolerable. Hardly anyone traveled on the roads this time of the morning. Roads were clear despite the snow that fell the night before. There were only a few patchy sections of ice here and there. Nothing much to speak of.

He made a right onto Madison, slowed down to go around a garbage truck making its morning pick-ups, then made a left on Reynolds Drive. He thought about picking up some donuts for the office, perhaps a sandwich for lunch since it was too cold to go out, but he thought better of it. He needed to lose a few pounds, and getting out, even in the cold, was a nice change from the monotony of his job. He took another sip of coffee, getting cold now, and placed the cup in the cup holder on the dash.

It happened in less than a second. Something crossed the road. A dog? A cat? He couldn't tell. He put his foot on the brake; the rear of the car spun around, just missing a telephone pole but bounced off a mound of snow piled up on the side of the road. The car stopped. He took a minute to compose himself then exited the car to check the damage. This must be his lucky day; not even a dent. Thank God. He held his coat tight to his chest, the wind picking up in intensity. He went back inside the car and started the engine. No one around. Too cold. He continued on his way to work.

At the end of the day, he headed home, stopping for Chinese food, and pulled into the garage. He placed the food on the kitchen counter, took off his coat, and went to the front door to gather his mail and evening paper. It was good to be inside. The office was kept at a cooler temperature than he liked, and his home was warm and welcoming. Off with his shoes and back into the kitchen, he looked through the mail and opened up the paper. He got a fork out of the drawer, sat down, put a forkful of fresh shrimp lo mein in his mouth, and started to choke. There on the front page of the paper the headlines read:

CHILD FOUND DEAD IN SNOW ON REYNOLDS
DRIVE POLICE LOOKING FOR WITNESSES

He continued to read:

A six-year-old girl was found dead in the snow. Exact time of death is undetermined at this time due to the freezing cold temperatures. Cause of death is unknown, but reports indicate that the small body was badly bruised. Police are seeking the help of anyone who may have seen anything unusual...

Oh, my God, he thought. *I was on that street.*

He remembered seeing something. He thought it had been a dog or cat. But a child? Why would a child be out in the streets that early in the morning? Could he have hit her and not realized it? He admitted to himself that he wasn't paying much attention. He got up and poured himself a drink. Killing a child.

Oh, God. Don't let it be true. What if someone saw me? Surely if they had, the police would be knocking on my door by now. I couldn't live with myself knowing I killed someone, let alone a child. I can't go to the police now. I left the scene of a crime.

No, wait a minute. I checked the damn car. I got out and checked the car! I didn't see any child.

He tried to calm himself. He poured another drink, then another. The liquor didn't seem to help. He thought of the consequences should he be found out. What if someone saw him and could identify him? There weren't many cars on the road; his red sports car would certainly stand out on a cold morning with no other vehicles present.

He started to sweat; his knees were weak. The liquor was going to his head, yet he poured himself another drink.

This can't be true; this can't be happening...

The thought of killing someone was more than he could handle. He wanted to vomit. He was dizzy. He went upstairs into his bedroom. He opened the closet door and reached up for the shoebox on the top shelf. The gun was still there. He kept it loaded in case of an emergency, and this certainly qualified as an emergency. One more drink. He took the gun and put it under his chin, barrel facing upward.

"God, forgive me." Then he pulled the trigger.

The headlines in the paper the following morning said nothing about a man killing himself for no apparent reason, leaving no suicide note. A man that was liked by his neighbors, parents deceased with one sister living in the same city.

But there was a small article on page seventeen that read:

DRIVER OF GARBAGE TRUCK CONFESSES
TO KILLING YOUNG GIRL AFTER LOSING
CONTROL OF TRUCK ON ICE

21
LUCKY, OR NOT, HERE I COME!

I had been working for the ASPCA rescue unit out of Port St. Lucie for seven years and the #1 rule you have to learn is never get attached to any of the animals and I never broke that rule… except once.

I was called out to rescue a little dog that had fallen over board, was attacked by a small shark and left to drown by his owners, subsequently giving him the name "Sharkbait"; "Sharkey" for short. I knew in the back of my mind there was something special about him, but I didn't find out just how special he was until several years later. Perspective adopters would come in to view the dogs and were immediately drawn to his cage. He certainly wasn't the pick of the litter, nor would he ever be "best in show." The scars of the shark attack were mostly healed except for his left ear, which was almost completely missing, and a gash right in the center of his nose giving him a "confused" look, but he was adorable nonetheless. As much as the adults and children were drawn to him, he would shy away huddling in the corner of his cage. This continued for several weeks until a little boy and his mother walked through the door.

It was as if Sharkey came to life. He sprang to his feet, running over to the boy, wagging his tail. It was a perfect match.

Years later, we received a drop-off from a local veterinary clinic just outside of Palm City. The kennel clerk carried a dog, wrapped in bandages and a blanket, back to the kennels and placed him gently into a cage. I read the file presented to me by the driver:

> *Police were called to the address of Ms. Patty Breen, her son, and live-in boyfriend, Mr. Casey Warren. Neighbors complained of fighting and the eight-year-old boy running out of the house shouting for help. Upon arrival we found Ms. Breen in the kitchen with a knife in her hand and her boyfriend lying on the kitchen floor. Medics were called. He was pronounced dead at the hospital three hours later. Ms. Breen stated that she and Mr. Warren were drinking, and an argument ensued at which time Mr. Warren began to strike the child, pushing him against the refrigerator and kicked him in the chest and groin. It was at that point that the family dog attacked Mr. Warren, allowing the boy to run from the house and neighbors called the police and ambulance. The boy was taken to the hospital for treatment of multiple cuts and bruises and released several hours later.*

Attached to the file was a report from the Palm City Veterinary Clinic:

> *Domestic, male dog dropped off by police for treatment of broken ribs, fracture to right hind leg, and bruises to chest. Owner surrendered dog to clinic for treatment and possible adoption.*

I walked back to the kennel and looked in on our new resident. He could barely move when I opened his cage.

"Hi, fella, so you were a hero? We'll try to find you a good home; if not, you can stay with us. We don't euthanize anyone here, especially heroes."

He lifted his head, and much to my surprise, I could see a funny little nose with a gash right in the center giving our new resident a very familiar "confused" look.

Within two months, Sharkey was back on his feet—well, three of them. Due to an infection his fractured leg had to be amputated, but this didn't slow him down one bit. He followed me around the kennel and greeted all the visitors and played with all the children. Every night, he was very content to return to his cage where he would remain until the next morning. We never closed the door to his cage. He had a routine. Up at dawn, out the back door to do his business and greet the meat delivery truck, where he was sure to get a special treat, back in to supervise the cleaning of the cages and then the distribution of the food. He never missed visiting hour or the children's story time. He was still the first dog the children would come to, but no one wanted to adopt a three legged, older, nose-scarred dog.

That is, until Mrs. Shephard.

She was an 83-year-old woman who came in to adopt a "quiet, old" dog. Normally, animals are not adopted out to anyone of such advanced years, but as soon as she walked in the kennel, Sharkey rushed to her side, wagging his tail and licking her extended hand. Love at first sight! Since the chances of Sharkey ever being adopted by anyone else were few and financial cut backs made euthanasia a future possibility, we let the adoption go through.

Mrs. Shephard leaned down and held her new companion's face in her two, fragile and gentle hands, and said, "I think I'm going to call you Lucky. Is that okay with you?"

His reply was a wag of the tail and a lick on her cheek. She didn't even seem to care that his nose was crooked or that he only had three legs. After all, with her cane she, too, had three legs.

So off they went and I closed the file on Sharkey, now Lucky, and I never saw him in the kennel again.

But my story doesn't end there. No, on the contrary, it just began.

As I mentioned, due to cut backs, many kennels were closing, policies were changing, and layoffs were inevitable. I moved to Jupiter Inlet into a small condo for senior citizens within a short walk to the water where I would go to sit and read passing the time of day. In truth, I missed work, and I missed all the animals. I actually thought about adopting a pet for myself but thought better of it. *Too old*, I thought.

Then, one day, I was reading the paper and in the lower, righthand corner was an article that caught my eye: "Companion Waited Until the Angels Came." I read on:

> *Mrs. Isabelle Shephard, 91, died yesterday after a long illness in her home, but she was never alone. Her dog, Lucky, stayed by her bedside throughout her illness. Neighbors stated Mrs. Shephard adopted the disabled dog eight years ago, and the two have been inseparable ever since. Three years ago, a burglar ransacked several units in the assisted living complex where she lived, but when he tried to enter her apartment, Lucky attacked the intruder, enabling Mrs. Shephard to call the police who apprehended him. The mayor later awarded Lucky a medal of heroism. Lucky has been transferred to the Jupiter ASPCA.*

I was about to break the #1 rule—I was about to get attached…

Who am I kidding? I *was* attached to that silly, torn-nosed, puppy the first moment I saw him. I was right. In the back of my mind, there was something special about that little ball of fur. He made others feel special, and by God, he made me feel special just thinking about him.

So, Lucky, get ready because here I come!

22
MONEY ISN'T EVERYTHING

I always found when I was alone on assignment in a small town, the best way to get the feel of an area and find out just who's who was to mingle with the locals at the neighborhood bar. This time, it was even more significant since I overheard a story about a man who claimed to have found a buried treasure. The two women sitting next to me were very pleased to fill me in with the details.

"As I was saying, Gladys, our librarian, could probably tell you all you want to know. She's been working at the library for about 35 years now, her mother before that. If you want to know about Jessie and his treasure, she's the one to ask."

"This man Jessie, is he still living around here?"

"Oh, for gosh sakes, nobody really believes in that old yarn. Like we said, Gladys should have some of the old stories about the coin Jessie found. But that was years ago, and Jessie is sort of, you know, light in the head; one short of a dozen, if you know what I mean."

It was obvious I wasn't going to get any further information, so I threw a double sawbuck on the bar, said my farewells to the ladies and made plans to see Miss Gladys first thing in the morning.

I don't think of myself as being stupid, but if there is money hidden out there someplace, then I sure as hell am clever enough to find it all.

"To be clever enough to get all the money, one must be stupid enough to want it."

- G.K. Chesterton

Gladys was not what I had expected. She was pleasant to look at, well dressed, and had a quickness to her step more like a teenager than someone of her age.

"Good morning," I greeted. "I'm Drake Marshall."

"I was expecting you, Drake," she said with a pleasant smile and songlike voice. "You're here about Jessie's treasure. News travels fast in a small town. You're not the only one who's been here to find it over the years, but no one has ever found another coin. Rumor has it that Jessie never really found the coin but had it from childhood all along." She got up from her desk and shook my hand. "I'll be glad to answer any questions you might have, though. What would you like to know?"

"Do you have any photographs of the coin he found or articles that were written at the time Jessie stated he found it? I don't suppose he's still living in the area. Do you know where he went?"

She walked back to her desk and returned handing me a folder with several pieces of paper and a map.

"I anticipated your questions, and yes, he still lives in the same old shack he lived in as a boy. I'm afraid his mind isn't too clear as to where he found the coin, Drake, and I'm not too sure he still has it, but if he does, he'll be happy to show it to you. He never let us take any pictures of it."

I looked through the clippings. The map was marked showing me how to get to Jessie's home.

"Surely, if there was a treasure, with more coins, Jessie would have moved closer to town. According to this map, he lives about 50 miles outside of town deep into the woods."

"That's right. Jessie doesn't care much for money. Let me know if you need anything else."

> *"I don't care too much for money, for money can't buy me love."*
>
> - John Lennon & Paul McCartney

After a quick but tasty lunch at the *Beans and Gravy Café*, I headed out for Jessie's place. Although far out of town, it was a beautiful and peaceful ride. Once halfway there, the road narrowed into dirt obviously seldom traveled, with leaves and branches hindering my way. The overhang of tree limbs blocked out the sun, making the shadows give a ghost-like appearance as I drove further into the woods. Finally, I came to a clearing with only a small outcropping of trees to the left and an old, dilapidated shack set deep into the trees to the right. My first thought was that no one who had found a treasure, no matter how small, would choose to live in such conditions. I almost turned around but for the sound of a dog barking and the sight of an old man waving towards me to come closer. So I drove up to a smiling man, a dog waging his tail, and the smell of coffee brewing. I didn't know how Jessie knew I was coming, but he welcomed me into his home. Although shabby, it was as clean as a whistle. His coffee was better than I had ever tasted, and his conversation was engaging. That is until I asked him about the treasure.

"I was a wondering just how long it was gonna take 'fore ya'll brought that up. Ya see I don't git many visitors up this ways but when I does, they always ask me 'bout my treasure. Why ya wanna know?"

"I'm here in town on business, and when I heard about the coin you found, I suppose I was just curious."

Jessie stood up and poured us another cup of coffee, sat down, and looked at me with smiling eyes. "Fer a man lookin' for treasure, ya should've brought yourself a shovel and worn some jeans instead a that fancy suit you're a wearing. Didn't them folks in town tell ya that I'm a little touched in the head? Ever think there might not be any treasure at all?"

I smiled, knowing that that was exactly what I was thinking.

"Well, that's quite possible but according to the paper clippings that Miss Gladys gave me there just might be some truth to the story. So tell me, did you find a treasure or not?"

"It's a gittin' late and soon it'll be too dark to see yourself back to town. Ya come back in the morn and maybe my dog Skeeter and I might show ya were I done found my treasure."

At the sound of his name, the dog jumped up and ran out the door to my car and barked as if to say "Goodbye, here's your hat—what's your hurry?"

I thanked Jessie for his hospitality, and before I drove away, I could hear him yell, "Don't forgit the shovel!"

I didn't know what tomorrow would bring, but I just couldn't believe there was any treasure. If there were, surely Jessie would be living in a home with running water, heat, a toilet, and certainly electricity. I do know that if I had a hidden treasure someplace, I'd have a mansion, new car and a beach house on some secluded island.

"If you want to know what the Lord God thinks of money, you have only to look at those to whom he gives it."

- Maurice Baring

The next day, I got up bright and early, got a donut and coffee at the café, then went down to the local hardware store. I was impressed to see just how well stocked it was. Not ever having done any manual labor, I picked up a pair of work gloves and chose a shovel with not too much weight and pointed at the end for best digging. I brought my items up to the counter and handed the clerk my credit card.

"Well, Mr. Marshall, I see Jessie got you hooked on hunting for buried treasure," the clerk said.

"I don't see how you people in town could possibly know that," I replied.

The clerk laughed as he looked towards my new purchases.

"Well, sir, I believe the shovel gave it away, plus the fact old Jess has a US Navy Shipboard two-way radio left over from WWII. About the only time he ever comes into town is to get batteries for the dang thing. That's how he keeps in touch with the outside world, so to speak." He handed me back my credit card. "Don't want to keep you, have a good day, and good luck."

With that, he went on to help another customer, and I went out to my car and drove off eating my donut with a grin on my face.

On the entire ride out to Jessie's, all I could think about was the gold coin. Maybe by tonight I just might be a millionaire!

> *"Money, it turned out, was exactly like sex. You thought of nothing else if you didn't have it and thought of other things if you did."*
>
> - James Baldwin

Jessie was waiting for me outside his home. I hesitate calling it that, but to him, it was a home, and apparently, he was anxious to get started.

"I'm ready to go but if you're a hankerin' for a cup a coffee 'fore we leave, I'll be glad to heat it up for ya."

"No, I'm ready," I replied.

For an old man, he certainly could keep up the pace. I was out of breath within 10 minutes. I could see he was disappointed in my physical condition but said nothing about it. Actually, he said very little as we traveled upward along the twisting path over rough terrain.

After some time, I asked, "How much farther?"

"We can take a break just up ahead a bit. I'll show you my coin when we's a sittin'."

"Don't tell me you carry it around with you?"

"I never leave it outta my sight. Keep it in my drawers, you know, my BVDs."

Skeeter reached the resting spot before we did, and I was glad to see that he seemed more tired than I. I waited just a few minutes before Jessie reached into his "drawers" and pulled out his coin and handed it over to me. If you had a feather, you could have knocked me over with it. There, in my hand, was a 1933 $20 Saint-Gaudens Double Eagle gold piece. My hand shook; my heart almost stopped. Suddenly, this was no longer a pleasant little walk in the woods to find a few little coins that may or may not exist. Jessie was no longer a half-wit hillbilly living in a worn-down shithole in the middle of nowhere. He was the only one standing between me and a fortune. I remembered reading about these coins and the big lawsuit and trial. The coins were never to be circulated and supposed to be destroyed, but a man in Philadelphia got hold of 10 of them. Years later, when his family tried to sell them, the government found out and stated the coins were illegal. The coins were confiscated and thus the trials began. One coin was said to be given to King Farouk and valued at near $8 million. Greed touched my soul. I was going to have that coin no matter what I had to do to get it.

> *"Let me tell you about the very rich. They are different from you and me."*
>
> - F. Scott Fitzgerald

I tried to hide my emotions.

"Do you think there are more coins hidden?"

"I have my doubts. Many others have come here, same as you, but they found nothin'. Let's git goin' an' ya can see fer yerself."

We walked about another two miles with Skeeter close behind until we came to a small clearing.

"Here it is," he said, "take a look see."

There was a hole in the ground about four feet wide and seven feet deep with piles of dirt, grass, and debris tossed to the side along with several shovels similar to mine.

"I see you really have taken others up here before me. Did they find anything?"

"I told ya, nothin'. Oh, they dug a little jist to satisfy themselves. Then we had a good laugh, shook hands, and they left. Said this gave 'em somethin' to talk 'bout."

Well, I was sure going to have something to talk about alright while I was spending all my money. All I had to do was get him in the right position, swing my shovel and knock him out. Then I'd take the coin, push him in the hole and cover him up, and off I'd go to live the life I was meant to lead. Now if I can just get him in the right position…

Just at that moment, Jessie moved and turned to the left as Drake swung the shovel. Skeeter ran over and jumped up, knocking Drake into the hole, hitting his head on a rock as he fell to the bottom.

Jessie walked over, looked into the hole, then looked over at Skeeter.

"Well, I'll be danged, think that poor fella is done dead." He smiled, picked up the shovel and started to pile dirt on top of Drake, saying, "Skeeter, that young man thought I was dumb, but I ain't that dumb."

The love of money is the root of all evil.
- The Bible

23
MANY QUESTIONS

The little Lakota child, often called Many Questions, sat watching his father, the Wise One, create a circle made of reeds and tiny strips of leather. As the Wise One quietly worked, the child asked questions as to what his father was creating. His father asked him to be patient; soon, he would discover what so carefully he was making.

"Father, please tell me the use for such a strange object."

The Wise One placed his creation on the dirt floor of the teepee.

"The Great Spirit's creations are all connected to the animals that give us life. For without them, there would be no people. This, my curious one, is a dream catcher." He picked it up and held it toward his son. "You see how it is made into a circle? The circle represents life. You see how the Sacred Spider has woven a tight web within the circle?" He pointed to the reeds he had woven around and inside the rim of the circle. "Look closely, and you will see a small hole in the center. The Sacred Spider has left this vacant space, he did not make a mistake."

The boy seemed disinterested in his father's explanation, and his little stomach was grumbling from hunger.

"But what is it for, Wise One?"

Patiently, his father explained.

"This dream catcher is placed over your bed of furs at night. As you dream, the good dreams are caught in the web to bring you peace while you sleep. The bad dreams pass through the hole, so they can not harm you."

"But why must we dream?"

"Dreams help us to see the future and understand the past. They are like a vision; they tell us a story."

"Father, what kind of story?"

"You ask too many questions. Run along, and we will discuss this another time when your belly and moon are full, and you are not so restless."

That night, the little Indian boy fell fast asleep. His sleep was troubled with many visions that he did not understand. The next day, he went to the Wise One and asked of his dream.

"Father, I dreamt about a little rabbit. Does that mean we will have plenty of food for our dinners during the winter moons?"

"The rabbit means that you are quick to conclusions. Being quick without thought leads to mistakes; mistakes that cannot be corrected."

The next night, he went to bed early, so that he could learn more about his dreams. This time, he dreamed about an owl.

"Father," he asked the next day. "Last night I saw an old owl flying in the sky but had difficulty doing so because of the wind. Does that mean that I will grow to be wise, like you?"

"No, it means that wisdom comes with age, but wisdom does not come easily. There are many obstacles in our way."

Many Questions was losing his patience. It was much too difficult to figure out what his dreams meant. The next time he saw his father, the Wise One asked him if he had any further dreams. When the boy answered no, he took him to the teepee of the oldest, wisest elder of the tribe. They called him the storyteller. He motioned the boy in and placed a hand on the pelts next to him motioning him to sit at his side.

"You ask about your dreams." He spoke very slowly and almost in a whisper. His face was worn and full of wrinkles and his eyes were looking at the boy but without sight. The boy waited for him to say more. Finally, the storyteller drew a circle in the dirt with a long, curved stick which had been stripped of its bark.

"This circle represents all of creation. All living things live inside this circle. When our people were very young, when buffalo roamed free on the land and fish were plenty in the seas, there was harmony between the people and the animals. Life was good."

He stopped speaking, and the boy moved closer to him, not wanting to miss a word. The storyteller then took a small, round stone from his totem and placed it in the center of the circle. He placed his fingers next to it and snapped them causing the marble to roll from the center to the outside of the circle, stopping about six inches beyond its rim, breaking the line of circumference.

"This small ball represents the 'Outsider,' the one who dreamed."

The storyteller then began to stand, leaning on the boy for support. His old body was weak, but his mind was strong. He took the boy's hand and brought him to the outside, where the air was cold and the sky was bright, and pointed to the stars and said, "Although I cannot see them, they are there. Do you see them clearly?"

"Yes!"

"Not all things are so clear. The Outsider was a great warrior who dreamed of being outside the circle, watching over and protecting the people. He said he saw visions in his sleep, and the visions told him of the future. He said he saw a great, dark tunnel destroying many of our people. He did not understand his dream but knew he must learn from it. Everyone laughed at him, for no one else ever had these 'sleeping visions.' He eventually became an outsider to the people as well as to himself.

"But one day, there was a great stillness that spread over the land. The sky turned gray, and Mother Earth trembled with such force, the earth began to crumble. Wind was powerful, destroying the trees, huts, and plantings for our spring harvest. Light came from the sky, lighting the holy mountain as the fires swallowed our homes and heated up the earth. When water fell from the sky, it filled the rivers overflowing their banks. The air turned cold, and the falling water turned to ice covering the land. Our people fled in confusion, not knowing which way to go. The wind turned into a spinning tunnel, picking up and throwing things about.

"The Outsider recalled the rest of his vision and knew what he had to do. He took his bow and rode to the top of the sacred hills, aiming his arrow into the swirling wind. The arrow flew through the air into the center of the storm. All at once, light began to break through the darkness, and the wind turned towards the Outsider still standing on the hill. The air remained cold. The people watched in wonder as the wind lifted him up and threw him outside the circle sending him into the unknown world of the stars."

The small boy asked, "Was the Outsider ever seen again?"

"Yes, my son. Look up. He is in the sky. The White Man has named him Orion."

24

NEW YEAR'S TRAGEDY

January 1, 2007

Baltimore Chronicle, Page 2

NEW YEAR'S TRAGEDY

Ringing in the New Year and making your New Year's resolutions does not always mean that the New Year is going to bring happiness. Mr. and Mrs. Joseph Brennan found that out after they partied just a little bit too much last night while attending a reception for E-Corp employees at the Hyatt Ballroom.

After leaving the Hyatt at 1:30 a.m., they headed home. Although the roads were free from any ice and snow, somehow they lost control of their 2005 Chevrolet Impala and ended up in a ravine alongside the road leading onto the Baltimore Expressway. They were taken to the hospital and are in critical condition.

January 15, 2007

Baltimore Chronicle, Page 8

WIFE DIES

Investigation continues into the unfortunate death of Mrs. Alice Brennan as a result of injuries sustained on New Year's Day. While returning from a party at the Hyatt, it appears her husband lost control of their vehicle, and both ended up in critical condition. Police questioned other party goers, who stated both Mr. and Mrs. Brennan did not drink anything more than gingerale that night. Further inquiry by authorities revealed nothing to be wrong with their car, although there were several skid marks apparent on the road. Visibility was good, according to weather reports.

Mr. Brennan continues to hold onto his life to the amazement of attending physicians.

The possibility of another vehicle being involved had been considered, but no evidence can substantiate the fact. Anyone having any information is requested to contact the Police Department at 555-555-1515.

Due to mounting medical bills, the family has had to mortgage their house. This reporter wonders, "Where is their insurance company?" Surely they had insurance.

February 26, 2007

Baltimore Chronicle, Page 19

BENEFITS DENIED ACCIDENT VICTIM

This reporter is looking into the denial of medical benefits due Mr. Brennan and his late wife by his no-fault insurance carrier. Because it has yet to be proven that Mr. Brennan was not driving under the influence at time of the incident, and that the incident remains under investigation, they are not under any obligation to pay any of the mutating medical bills. Mr. Brennan's employer, E-Corp, is one of the leading pharmaceutical companies in the US with companies expanding worldwide, and their healthcare carrier, Dependable Care Health Insurance, is refusing benefits to Mr. Brennan and his late wife as a result of injuries sustained on New Year's Eve.

Controversy over whether or not Mr. Brennan paid his January premium remains an issue, but Attorney Lemson, now retained by Mr. Brennan's sister, asks how he would pay the premium if he is lying unconscious in the hospital? This reporter asks the same question.

Although witnesses say the Brennans were not drinking alcohol, the question remains as to whether or not they had been drinking and whether or not the hotel is responsible for serving too much liquor to someone who might have been drunk. The Hyatt Hotel claims they did not supply the caterer or bar attendant for this party; therefore, they are not responsible.

Regardless of who is responsible, Mrs. Brennan is dead, and Mr. Brennan remains in critical condition, receiving very little care due to lack of responsibility of any party to pay the medical bills.

March 1, 2007

Baltimore Chronicle, Page 24

HOSPITALS WON'T HELP DYING MAN

It is hard to believe in this day and age that someone would be left to die in a hospital because no one claims responsibility for the bills.

So is the case with Mr. Brennan who, two months ago, was in an accident entering the Baltimore Expressway.

Attorney Lemson has been retained to look into this tragic situation since no one is stepping forward to claim responsibility for the thousands of dollars' worth of medical bills for both he and his wife resulting in injuries sustained on New Year's day. Mr. Lemson has tried, without success, to get either the car insurance or private healthcare carrier to pay any of the bills. In the meantime, Mr. Brennan remains in a coma, fighting off pneumonia and several bouts of infection and heart failure.

Physicians say they are amazed at how long Mr. Brennan has held on due to the severity of his injuries. Several organizations have donated blood and funds to help obtain treatment for Mr. Brennan. Several doctors have donated their services in order to help a patient who apparently has been abandoned by the health care system.

March 5, 2007

Baltimore Chronicle, Page 31

OBITUARY

Mr. James T. Brennan died today after a long illness. Mr. Brennan was survived by a sister, Harriet Cummings, and niece Kathy, who lived with the deceased. Services will be held at the Long Funeral Home in Middle River on Wednesday, March 7 from 1:00 to 3:00 in the afternoon and 6:00 to 8:00 in the evening.

In lieu of flowers please make donations to your charity of choice.

May 1, 2007

Court Decision

Baltimore County

DECISION

The Baltimore County Court System has found both the insurance company and hospital negligent and direct cause of the death of Mr. and Mrs. Brennan. Both Mr. and Mrs. Brennan were denied benefits from both their car insurance and health providers, resulting in lack of effective and aggressive treatment by the Hospital. Damages in the amount of $75,000 were awarded the family.

September 3, 2008

Baltimore Chronicle, Back Page

UPDATE

This reporter followed the plight of Mr. and Mrs. Brennan since their fatal accident on January 1, 2007. After a long and heartbreaking trial their attorney, Mr. Lemson won the case having been awarded $75,000 from the insurance company and hospital. However, after the conclusion of the case the manufacturer was found negligent and an additional settlement of $5,000,000 was awarded the family.

25
REFLECTIONS IN THE MIRROR

It happened in less than a second, the shrieking sound of tires, a body twisting at the force of impact, and the other sound—the horrible sound of metal crushing against bone. Then there was silence, then darkness.

Shelby delayed getting out of bed. Her recurrent dreams were becoming more vivid and frightening. She rolled over and curled herself up under the warmth of the blankets and looked at the picture on her bedside table of a man and woman heavy with child. The picture had been taken at a happier time that now seemed never to have existed.

Her present life wasn't so bad. She had a beautiful home and a well-paying job doing freelance work at home since working outside the home was out of the question. She couldn't cope with the stares, turning of heads, and whispered comments. Preparing for the day ahead of her should be easy. But at least once during the preparation, she saw herself in the mirror, and what she saw there was what she refused to see in her dreams.

She got up and slowly walked to her desk. Today, she decided to write in her journal about that day and how the carelessness of a drunk driver took away her child and her beauty. She would tell all her feelings, her pain, and her anger.

As Shelby continued to write, the angrier she became, and she made a decision. She would confront him. Yes, she was going to confront the man who abandoned her and the child she once carried.

She remembered his name and every inch of his face, how he walked, smelled, and the feel of his kiss, ever so tender. She'd loved him once. She thought he'd loved her. At first, she hadn't blamed him for being drunk, crashing the car, and leaving the scene, but during the many months of rehab, she never saw him again. He never came to share the grief of losing the child they had created together. How much better off she would have been to die there. Instead, her life continued.

Shelby was no longer a woman of grief. She was a woman who wanted revenge. She wanted him dead.

Before closing her journal, she made one last entry: "It will not be difficult to find him, and before I take his life, I want him to see the same torn, disfigured horror I see every day when I look into the mirror."

As she entered his building, she began to have doubts. The place was dark and dusty, with paint peeling from the ceiling. This was certainly not where the wealthy man she knew would have chosen to live. Her heart was pounding, and she began to shake. The gun shifted in her pocket as she entered the dingy hallway. As her eyes adjusted to the darkness, she noticed only a few pieces of furniture were present. There was a sterile odor and a strange beeping sound in an otherwise quiet room. The sound was familiar. Not a comforting familiarity. She gripped the gun tighter as she called his name.

"Jonathan, it's Shelby. I thought I would surprise you with a visit long overdue."

There was no answer. The beeping sound was now deafening. Her head began to pound. Then she saw him, lying in bed, lifeless, pale. Tubes and machines were hooked up to his still, fragile form. He looked unconscious. She advanced closer and noticed a picture of a beautiful man and a woman on the small table next to his bed. It was the same picture she woke up to every morning. His features were almost the same, much thinner with a little less hair, now gray, but still handsome except for his stare. There was no recognition or reaction as she stood over him, ready to pull the trigger to end his life.

He couldn't see how terrifying her face was. He was a vegetable as a result of the same terrifying accident that took away her beauty. She whispered, "No wonder you never came to see me. You don't even know about the death of our child. What sort of revenge would there be by me pulling the trigger now?"

She let go of the gun and placed it back in her pocket. She walked over to the small table, took the dusty picture frame, and removed the picture and tore it up. She let the pieces fall onto the dusty floor. Then, she turned to walk from the room, and as she reached the door, she heard him say: "I'm sorry."

Without turning, she replied, "So am I."

It was time to forgive. There was no need for revenge. As she continued to walk down the darkened hall, she stopped in front of a mirror. Slowly, she turned and looked at herself. What reflected back at her was a beautiful woman with skin of ivory and eyes the color of sapphires. Forgiveness set her free.

26
THE BEAUTY OF A MEMORY

She was no longer able to drive since her eyesight had gotten worse, so she took a cab to the bank. She slowly exited the cab, one weak leg at a time. Her steps were slow with a slight limp. Her hunched, arthritic posture was that of an old woman, but in her heart, she was only 23. In her mind, she was still beautiful.

The security guard opened the door, addressing her by her full name. Everyone at the bank knew her. She came there once a month to cash a check. "For miscellaneous expenses," she would say. She'd take the money, put it in her small, worn purse then awkwardly walk to the elevator, press the down button, and patiently wait for the elevator to take her to the vaults.

At the manager's desk, she signed the necessary papers and was given a key. Once in the vault, she went over to safe deposit box number 372, put in the key, then took out a tin box. It wasn't very heavy, and she was easily able to bring it over to the table provided. Her hands trembled as she removed her gloves and her wide-brimmed hat, placing them alongside the box. She took another key in her feeble fingers and painfully opened the box. Inside were some old papers and photos of a time long past; a time that, in her mind, was only yesterday. A long, black, velvet case rested under the papers. She gently took it out and removed the lid. Her eyes closed as her heart skipped a beat in anticipation.

A string of identically matched pearls rested inside the case. These were the pearls her husband had given her on their wedding day over 65 years ago. She could feel his fingers, even now, rough from years of hard work, caressing her neck as he fastened the gold clasp around her neck. The thrill of his touch was just as exciting to her now as it had been those many years ago.

All at once, she was young again. Hair no longer gray but filled with a golden sheen that bounced as she tossed her head from side to side. Her own hands felt the perfectly round pearls. Hands now smooth with skin of ivory. She quickly stood, holding out her arms as if dancing in the wind, clinging to some invisible lover. No longer did her legs feel the pain of age. Instead, they glided across the floor to the tempo of music only she could hear. A tear fell down her cheek of flawless beauty, a smile on her red lips.

She could feel his warm kiss, the faint whisper of his breath as he said, "I love you"; his tender touch; his heart beating against her breast. She didn't need a mirror to show her she was beautiful. All she needed were her memories.

Soon, it was time to go. She put the necklace back in the case, placing it under the papers, and closed the safe deposit box, returning it back into slot number 372.

The employees of the bank were always amazed at how quickly she left the bank, how much happier she seemed to be, how much more confident in her step she was. No one ever spoke to her as she left. Even if they did, she would never have heard them. She was no longer there—she was in another time, a time when she was beautiful.

27
THE BRACELET OF LIFE

2008

Dr. James Arnold sat waiting in Dr. Michael Artz's office wondering why he was requested to come here today. Dr. Artz was late, and James was just about to leave when the doctor walked in, extending his hand.

"Sorry to keep you waiting, I was held up in the lab. I've heard so much about your research on tissue growth that I wanted to see you as soon as I could."

"Thank you, Dr. Artz, but when the government took away my funding, I'm afraid my research was put on hold."

"Please, call me Mike. I hope that after our meeting today, you will accept my offer and continue your research. Come with me for a tour of my laboratory. I hope you will find it interesting enough to become part of the team."

James was surprised by his comments and curious as to what he had to offer.

"Keep an open mind," he told himself.

Both men walked out the door without further comment. Perhaps curiosity got the better of James, so like a little puppy dog, he followed him down a long, dimly lit corridor. After passing several doors and through many passages, they arrived at what he assumed must be the lab. Dr. Artz took a passkey from his pocket, placed it in the slot, pressed in a code, and the door opened. James took several steps before he actually comprehended what he was seeing. The room was about 60,000 square feet with what appeared to be hundreds of technicians all busily at work. Towards the back and sides of the room were cylinders, all the same size, approximately seven feet high.

Dr. Artz was the first to speak.

"I know this is a lot to take in all at once, but when I explain to you what it is we do here, I'm sure you will understand."

"To have such a massive space for research is impressive. I'm used to working in a lab about the size of your bathroom and a staff too small to even count on one hand. You definitely have my attention."

"Good, that's what I had hoped. Come. Look over here. This is where the research begins, in these test tubes. We've moved several steps beyond cloning a rodent or sheep. We are cloning a human body. But not for the purpose of increasing the population or making a more intelligent being. We are growing bodies for organ transplantation."

James could not have been more surprised or stunned.

"I don't understand. Are you saying all these cylinders contain a human being? One you intend to destroy for the purpose of supplying someone else with an organ taken from that body? You must be crazy. How would I fit into all this?"

"No, James. These bodies we are growing will not be able to process thought because they have no brain. They possess only the necessary body components to grow organs to the point where their organs can be harvested for transplant. Once an organ is removed, we will have the capability of growing another one inside the same host. There is no emotion, no thinking or stimuli that would put them in the category of being considered 'human.' At this point in time, they are just for experimentation."

"How many of them are there? You still haven't told me where I fit in."

"So far we have 57 'cadavers,' as we call them. Each are given a bracelet identifying them not by name but when they were created and the expected date their organs can be harvested. And where do you fit in? Your research on skin grafting and growth of tissue from a dead cadaver into living cells is astounding. You see, if we could create an artificial skin, such as what you were working on, then our cadavers would be able to grow twice as fast, making the organs ready to transplant even sooner. People are waiting too long for a transplant. Companies are making it much too difficult to obtain the necessary organs and charging a fortune. With our process, there would be no need to find a match. These cadavers would be a perfect match for anyone, regardless of sex, blood type, or age. The fact that our cadavers are free of any disease makes it unnecessary for pre-testing. There are individuals willing to pay anything for a heart or kidney, regardless of how they are obtained. Let's face reality, the person with the most money gets the first available organ. The rich don't have to be placed on a waiting list. My process would eliminate all that."

James couldn't believe what he just heard, although he did not disagree…entirely. He walked over to one of the cylinders and looked through the viewing glass. He could see what he thought to be a woman in her early twenties. The bracelet she wore read: "Donor #3721—Creation: 1998—Termination: 2012." There was a red light flashing on her bracelet, indicating she was not ready to be harvested. Her body was so…serene. How could she not have feelings? Somehow, he felt a connection with her. How could she only be considered a host waiting to be dissected and distributed at the will of some mad man? He looked down the room—57 bodies without any memories or someone to love them.

"Dr. Artz, I don't see how I can help you. If it takes 14 years for a body to mature, I don't see how any of my research can help you. "

"I know you must be overwhelmed, but if you or a loved one needed an organ transplant, wouldn't you want one as soon as possible? You would not want to watch that loved one deteriorate to the point of non-recognition and then only lose them because a donor was never available. You have an opportunity to be a part of something great, something that will help hundreds or even thousands of people."

"I'm sorry, but ethically, I can't help you. My research is years behind your research here. It would probably take me 10-15 years to catch up, even with the help of your impressive staff. I appreciate the faith you have placed in me, but I can't help you."

"Perhaps you'll change your mind, which I hope you do, once you have had time to think about it. My assistant will show you the way out."

2012 — Community General Hospital

James looked down at his seven-year-old daughter, frail from years of pain and inactivity. She was born with a hole in her heart; "minor," the doctors had said, but it turned out to be more than minor. Test after test showed no improvement. Doctor after doctor offered no solution.

But today would be different. He and his wife labored long and hard to make the decision for a heart transplant, hoping her heart would heal itself. Today, yes, today would change her life to a better life, letting her have the childhood she never had.

He watched as they prepared her for surgery and rolled her down the hall into the operating room. The doctor, dressed in scrubs and mask, looked at James and nodded, indicating everything would be fine; there was nothing to worry about.

He stayed there looking at the closed door for some time. The hours passed as his own heart beat silently in prayer. He would have gladly changed places with his daughter and made a deal with the devil when a nurse came up to him and handed him an envelope.

"The doctor asked me to give you this when the surgery was over. Everything went well and you will be able to see your daughter in a few minutes."

Tears fell from his face as he opened the envelope. Wrapped in pink tissue paper was a bracelet: "Donor #3721— Creation: 1998—Termination: 2012."

28

THE BUREAU

Caroline, 28 years of age, was here because of her mother's daily journal. Since her grandmother's death, she spent a lot of time cleaning out her things. Over the years, they lost touch until one day she received notice of her death. Coming back home was difficult but necessary. There wasn't much of any value, only some sentimental items with the rest being given to charity. Then, one day, stuffed in the bottom of an old sailor's shipping trunk, she found her mother's journal. Whether or not her grandmother even knew of its existence, she didn't know, but once she started to read it, she found it hard to put down.

January, 1924

Today my dear husband gave me such a beautiful gift made of maple, a bureau to celebrate our first-year anniversary. The top is as smooth as glass with a shine only outdone by the sun. There are four drawers with knobs of ivory. On one of the drawers, he has carved a beautiful rose; he knows how much I love them. There is but one stem void of thorns. He joked that I would never prick myself on this rose as I have done so many times in my garden. I asked why he only carved one rose— the other drawers seemed so bare in comparison. He smiled, leaned down, kissed my cheek and replied, "The rest are yet to come."

So, here she was, sitting in her car in the driveway of an old mansion owned by the late Honorable Grey Shandler. The estate was being auctioned off, piece by piece, by his son, Colin.

She exited her car and went up the 30-some-odd steps to the front entrance, where she was given her paddle #47.

"You may view all the items on the second floor, but only the contents in the living room and library are up for bid on the main floor. Please do not enter the other rooms since they are off limits. The third-floor rooms have not been utilized for the past 30 years and are in some disarray, so please watch your step and ask for assistance if you are interested in any item and want a closer look. Here is a brochure, although not complete, that you might want to refer to as you peruse the various rooms. Please stay within the corded off areas. Thank you for your cooperation and your attendance in today's auction."

All this was said in less than 30 seconds by someone who was obviously bored and had said it many times before.

Caroline didn't know what to expect but certainly not what she saw once inside the foyer. She had a feeling of stepping back in time. She could imagine people milling around in their gowns and dinner jackets, enjoying the music coming from the music room off to the right.

She walked into the dining room and saw a Chippendale, solid mahogany dining table with silver gilt tortoiseshell inlaid flowers and birds that filled most of the room, easily seating 30 guests. The chairs, also of mahogany, were covered in brocade with the same pattern. The table was set, as if guests were to arrive at any moment, with Red Rose porcelain, Venetian crystal, and thistle patterned silverware. The table was covered in fine linen trimmed with handmade lace, napkins to match.

Although beautiful, she could see a thin layer of dust covering the items, representing a long time of non-use.

Caroline proceeded to the second floor. This is where she hoped to find what her mother so cherished.

May, 1926

> *The weather is very warm with just a slight breeze making the flowers in the garden dance in the sun. Tonight, I will tell my husband that I am expecting a child. I know he will want a son, but should it be a girl, I know he will love and spoil her as he has loved and spoiled me.*

Caroline reached the top of the stairs, turned left, and looked into one room after another. All were beautifully decorated in the finest available for its time with portraits on the walls of long-gone ancestors of the Shandler family. The bedrooms were furnished with crisp, white linen, and the window coverings were heavy tapestries blocking out the light.

Then she came to the library filled with rows and rows of first editions covered in leather with gold embossed lettering. Cobwebs covered most of the books except for a few that were placed on a desk in the far corner. If the Shandlers only read one-hundredth of this collection, it would be more than she could read in a lifetime.

February, 1927:

> *Another rose has been added to my treasured bureau. This one is smaller than the last representing the little girl born to us just one month ago. We have named her Dianne. It is strange how such a tiny bundle can make such a change in our lives. I could not ask for a better life.*

As Caroline was leaving the library, a man approached her and introduced himself.

"I'm Colin, Grey Shandler's son. You must be Caroline. You look much like your mother."

"You knew my mother?"

"I knew of her. At one time, my father had several pictures of her throughout the house. Did you know she and your father worked for him for many years? Although she was one of the many servants, she was always special to my father. When she died, I believe a part of him died with her. Enough of my reminiscing. Are you here to bid on something special or just looking?"

"It's nice to meet you, Mr. Shandler."

"Please call me Colin."

"To be honest, Colin, I'm not quite sure. I found my mother's journal among my grandmother's things. In it, there were several notations about a carved bureau. I suppose I was curious enough to come today and see it for myself, if you still have it. It was not among my grandmother's things, so I thought it might be here."

"Ah, the bureau." He sighed, looked down for a moment then regained his composure. "It may be somewhere, but I doubt it is in the main part of the house. Probably on the third floor with all the other dust collectors. It was not one of my father's favorite pieces."

"Why do you say that?"

"You should finish reading the journal. You may find the answer to your question there. Perhaps I will see you before you leave. Good day."

Then off he went, leaving Caroline wondering what mysteries lay in the remaining pages of her mother's journal.

February, 1933

*This time I do hope I produce a son for my husband.
We have one beautiful daughter, the apple of her
father's eye, but I believe he still yearns for a son.*

October, 1933

*Another girl, the third rose. We have named her
Caroline. Joy fills our lives in many ways but one.*

Caroline decided to take Colin's advice and went to the
third floor. Indeed, everything was covered in dust. Pictures
were hanging awkwardly on the walls with chairs piled high,
one on top of the other. Most items were in need of repair;
some beyond repair. There were boxes in the far corner holding
worn and faded drapery and linens, and some contained broken
China and imported pottery. Lamps were set on the floor, in
no particular order, but she could see they were probably too
damaged to be functional. She looked way in the back, under
the one window, where she saw what she had come to see.

Cautiously, she walked towards the window and put out her
hand and gently stroked the bureau, stained and tilted to the
side and missing two of its legs.

December, 1939

*It is almost time to give birth. The doctor says it will
be a difficult delivery, and he hopes that this is my
last pregnancy. My health is not as it should be. I
fear the worst. My husband has once again carved a
fourth rose into the chest of drawers. This one more
beautiful than the rest. He still hopes for a son. He
knows this is our last chance. I love him so, but*

*things don't always seem as they are. I wish I could
put on paper the way I feel at this moment when
pain comes, and I wish for release of my guilt that
has caused sadness when this should be a blessing. I
hope he can forgive me.*

"I see you have found the bureau," Colin said as he walked
toward Caroline.

Deep in thought, she was startled when she heard his voice.

"Yes, even with all the damage, it is a work of art. Much
love went into its making. I only wish I got to know my mother
better. I was almost seven when she died. She died giving birth.
A son, who also died. See there," she said, pointing to the fourth
rose. "Grandmother told me that after mother and my brother
died, my father took a knife and cut through the rose leaving it
in pieces. Shortly after, he died of a broken heart."

Colin looked sad, a tear falling from his cheek falling onto
his Edwardian jacket.

"If that is what your grandmother told you, then she was
mistaken. You will excuse me please. If you want the bureau,
you may have it. It is a gift from me to you." With that, he left
the room, and Caroline could hear his heavy footsteps going
down the hall.

She left the mansion with one thought in mind. She must
finish reading the journal. Why would a perfect stranger give
her such a valuable gift?

January, 1940

*My heart is heavy with guilt. I do love my husband
so, but I was tempted by lust and the excitement at
the chance of wealth. Grey was so handsome and
convincing, but I knew it was a mistake. A mistake
that resulted in a child; a son. My husband is a*

loving man, an honest man. He did not deserve this deceit. I must tell him the truth before it is too late. I hope he has forgiveness in his heart.

February, 1940

My husband took a knife to my precious bureau, marring the last beautiful rose. To him, this child does not exist. He took the same knife and ended his own life. The shame of what I have done is too great for me to live with. I know my mother will take care of my two beautiful daughters. Grey Shandler will take and love our son, who I have named Colin. I shall weep no more, for it is time for me to lay at rest at the side of my beloved husband.

Caroline finished reading the last entry in her mother's tear-stained journal. She closed the pages and laid it in her lap. After a time of meditation, she stood and walked over to the bureau gently caressing each rose with her fingertips. When she came to the marred rose, she bent down and kissed it. She had many questions that would now remain unanswered, but it was now clear to her why Colin had given her the beautiful piece of furniture. With the journal in her hand, she ran to her car and headed off, hoping to see the mansion one last time. As she drove up the driveway, she could see the moving vans being loaded up and supervising the loading was Colin.

She pulled up closer and waved to him, and she parked the car.

Caroline looked into his troubled face.

"How long have you known?" she asked.

"Always. There were no secrets in our house. My father loved your mother very much. He spoke of her many times. As I said, he kept pictures of her throughout the house. He found comfort in seeing her face. It wasn't until I was about 14 that I first found the bureau in the attic. When I asked my father about the beautiful piece and why the one rose was so terribly destroyed, he told me what had happened. I had planned on having it repaired after my father died, and when I visited your grandmother and told her my plan, she asked that I destroy the piece, not to repair it, since it no longer brought happiness, only sorrow. I later found out my father sent your grandmother monthly checks to help support you and your sister. He continued to do so until the day he died. Despite what happened after my birth, I assure you that my father loved your mother, and for a time, she loved him as well. But in reality, she loved her husband more."

Caroline looked into his face, now more relaxed as if a weight had been lifted from his shoulders.

"Would you like to read the journal?"

He shook his head.

"The only good thing that has come from that journal is that now you have found me. I have always wanted a sibling, and having a sister is a dream come true."

She reached out and took his hand.

"My father was a good man. I know that if he had given himself time to grieve, he would have loved you as his own son. Your father was a good person, and he has raised a man who I am proud to call my brother."

29
THE EYE WITNESS

She woke up to the sound of seagulls flying low over the water, looking for their morning meal with the waves breaking over and caressing the sand. The sun's rays sparkled across her pillow onto her face. She slowly stretched, getting the kinks out of her system before placing her feet on the cool floor, then stood and walked to the bathroom, where she washed up, taking no more than 10 minutes. There was no need for makeup, and a quick comb through her hair was enough. She had put out her clothes the night before, always in shades of blue, gray, black, or white, not having to worry about matching. She slipped her feet into an old pair of sandals, put her glasses on, and went downstairs.

She lived in a modest cottage near the beach. The upstairs consisted of her bedroom and bathroom. Downstairs held her eat-in kitchen, living room, half-bath, and an art studio she hadn't used in some time.

The coffee pot had been pre-set for when she came downstairs. Breakfast consisted of a dry slice of toast and a very hot cup of coffee, which she took with her through the back screen door and down the wooden stairs, stopping several times to listen to children playing on the beach, dogs chasing balls, and everyday sounds that are often missed. Although she lived on "private" ocean front property, she was well aware of the early morning traffic of people passing through to get their spot on the beautiful beach only a few yards away.

She walked to the end of the dock and sat down on the warped boards, letting her feet dangle, swinging in the air with only her toes touching the water. It was happening again. She could feel it. Something was going to happen. She heard a loud noise and could hear someone running. She stood up and started to return to the house. She sipped her coffee; the air was suddenly cooler.

I should have brought a jacket, she thought.

All at once, someone bumped her, spilling her coffee and almost knocking her into the water. She heard a splash, then someone running down the dock and jumping off onto the sand, a scream, a car door slam, and tires squealing. There seemed to be confusion on the beach, but she couldn't tell what was happening. As quickly as she could, she returned to the cottage and decided it would be best to stay in today.

She was in the living room the next morning when she heard someone knocking on her door. She wasn't surprised. She was an eye witness, after all. But was she?

"Anna, are you there? I missed seeing you at the dock this morning. Are you okay?"

Anna sat up putting on her glasses. Jane Brown was her neighbor and landlord for over 10 years, but they were friends ever since the accident. Jane kept an eye on her and, at times, was more like a mother than a friend. Anna felt this was going to be one of those times.

"Yes, I'm okay. I was just resting. Thought you might be the police. Come on in."

Jane walked in and went directly toward Anna.

"Police? Why would you think they would be coming up here? Did something happen?"

"Something 'happened' yesterday when I was on the dock. It's happening again you know. They didn't believe me before, and I knew they won't believe me this time either. The difference is, I'm not going to them; they'll come to me."

Jane took a deep breath before she spoke. If it was happening again, that meant they were both in for a rough time.

"Anna, I believe you truly think what you see is real. Try to relax. I'll stay here, and later we'll have a little lunch. You'll see things differently, I promise."

"No, and don't treat me like a child. I know you mean well, but this time was different. I didn't 'see' anything, but I felt it. Something happened at the beach. If you won't believe me, then how can I expect the police to believe me? So I'm going to wait for them to come knocking on my door."

Sure enough, just as she was about to take her coffee and toast down to the dock, she heard a persistent knock at her door. "Well" she thought, let the show begin!"

Two police officers stood just outside the screen door introducing themselves as Detectives Simmons and Vellenti. They stated there was an incident at the beach next to her dock and would like to come in and ask her a few questions.

"I've been waiting for you, please, come in."

Simmons and Vellenti looked at each other, thinking, *This is going to be some interview.*

Simmons pulled a pad and pen from his back pocket and motioned for Anna to sit down.

"I understand from your neighbor that you are Miss Anna Campbell?"

"Yes."

"And you say you have been waiting for us. Why is that?"

"I am sure you did some inquiries about me before you came to my door. Therefore, you know the answer to that question."

"I'm not here to play 20 questions with you, but, yes, we routinely do background checks on people we are going to question, and it is noted that a few years ago, you called the police claiming you had been walking on the beach when someone struck you on the head, but when the police investigated there were no witnesses who saw anyone else on the beach other than yourself, and there were no footprints on the beach other than your own. How do you explain that, Ms. Campbell?"

Anna raised her head up to the detective and slowly removed her glasses, revealing a blankness only common to those that had not seen the joy of light, only darkness for a long time.

"I can't explain the absence of footprints on the beach other than my own. Can you explain my absence of sight ever since that day? I certainly didn't hit myself in the head. Since that time, I have felt visions that were going to happen, and when I called the police, they don't believe me, just as you won't believe me now."

It was Vellanti who spoke this time, but with a calmer tone.

"A child was kidnapped this morning, and her mother was killed. Just what was it you felt yesterday when you were on the beach?"

"I was actually on the dock." She closed her eyes. "The air was colder than usual, so I decided to get a jacket when I heard a gunshot, then someone came running towards me. It was a large person, at least 6' with an unusual gait. When he bumped into me, his arm brushed up against mine, and it was rough, not like a woman's. He smelled like cigar smoke. When he turned to get around me, it seemed he was carrying something heavy, which might account for his altered gait, because after I heard the splash, his gait was normal when he ran past me back up the dock and jumped back onto the beach, running towards the road. A woman had screamed and then I heard a door slam and tires squeal. It wasn't a car door; it was the type of side door on a van. It was heading towards Route 84. Must have been at least two people because the man that was running wasn't the driver. I could hear the car moving before the door closed."

"Thank you for your help, Ms. Campbell. If we have any further questions, we'll give you a call."

The two detectives left Anna's cottage with more questions than when they went in. Investigation did reveal the tire tracks were headed towards Route 84, and witnesses said they saw a green van parked on the causeway but couldn't say for sure if it was the same van seen on the beach. But what they did find was a cigar butt on the side of the causeway where the green van had been seen. Witnesses said the plates were out of state with a "From Hell and Back" sticker on the back fender.

"A splash in the water," she'd said, so they decided to check it out and called the police diving team. Seven hours later, the team found a pink sneaker and blanket that belonged to the missing girl but no sign of the body. The search would continue the next morning.

Jane came over to see Anna the next morning, bringing the *Daily News* with her.

"Anna, you're in the paper as an eye-witness. Funny, right? Anna, what's wrong? You look terrible. They never mentioned your name, so don't worry."

"They know who I am. The child is dead, probably washed out to sea and will never be found, but if they find the guy or guys, they can't make an arrest for the murder of the girl's mother. I'm afraid to go down to the dock. I feel trapped here."

"Don't be ridiculous. The police are all over the beach. They are keeping an eye on everyone. They even checked out my ID. I have to go to the store, need anything?"

"No, but thanks. Are you sure the police are on the beach?"

"Yes, even that cute Detective Vellanti. I'll check on you later."

Anna walked down the hall into her studio. She was once a gifted sculptor, but since the accident, she had packed up all her tools. She felt it was finally time to get rid of them; give them to some student who could benefit from them. She pushed aside some books and placed a box of clay on the table, opened it up, and was surprised to see it was still moist. She sat down; it was happening again. She felt a chill, and not realizing what she was doing, before she knew it, she was digging her fingers into the clay just as if she could see every crack and crevice. She also didn't realize that someone was opening her back screen door.

A sound woke her from her dream-like trance.

"Jane, is that you? I'll be right out." She cleaned off her fingers, never looking at what she had sculpted, and went out into the kitchen. Only she never made it beyond the doorway.

She screamed several times before the fatal stab wound silenced her cries, but they were heard by the detective patrolling the beach, who saw the man fleeing from her house. Although the child was never found, he was arrested and sentenced to life in prison for the deaths of Anna, the child, and her mother.

Several months after the trial, Jane went into the cottage to clean out Anna's belongings and make it ready for a new tenant. When she walked into the studio, she uncovered the piece of sculpture Anna had been working on the day she had died. There was a statue of two men and a woman. One man was obviously Anna's attacker with a knife in his hand, and the woman was Anna, falling to the ground, crying out with her eyes wide open with an awareness in them that Jane had never seen before. The other man was smiling holding a small child wearing one pink sneaker. In his other hand he held a card that read "Happy Father's Day."

Jane picked up the phone and dialed the police.

"Detective Vellanti speaking."

"This is Jane Brown calling. I just received a message from Anna. She knows where the child is."

30

THE FORGOTTEN

The two watched through their front window as the old woman once again walked down the street pushing her cart. They had seen her many times, curious as to her status, but never actually approached her. In the warmer weather, she wore a bandana of different colors, and in the cooler months, a babushka covered her head. Her skirt was dark and long, covering her thin legs. The cart she pushed was like those used in a smaller department store and carried the many items she had picked up on her walks around the neighborhood: boxes, cans, sticks, pieces of treasure added to her collection.

Although there was no verbal communication between them, a bond began to form. Whether it was from curiosity or concern, the mystery about this lost soul grew until one day, while working in her front yard, one of the watchers smiled and said, "Hello," to the old woman.

And so it began, a conversation, long overdue. The woman was so eager and pleased to speak that it was obvious she hadn't had someone to talk to in a long time. Even though her speech was difficult to understand, the watchers felt she was a gentle woman who had been left to the mercy of some uncaring caregiver. Her arms revealed bruises and scars, both old and new.

Time passed with no communication until, one day, the elderly woman stopped and dug deep down into her cart, pulling out a bag with several small, oddly shaped tomatoes.

"These are for your mother, please give them to her." With that, she continued on her walk to wherever she felt she had to go.

The next afternoon, the two watchers looked as the woman passed by. They waited until she was well down the block before following, careful not to be seen. It was several blocks before the woman stopped to pick some flowers from a neighbor's garden. She brought the flowers to her nose taking in their fragrance before putting them into her cart and continuing on her way up to Norton Street. After another block, she stopped in front of a two-story, brick house, immaculately landscaped. The two watched and witnessed a change in the old woman. She began to slump, her head bent to her chest and her hands fell to her side. A few moments passed before she reached into a pocket, bringing a tissue to wipe the tears from her cheek. She placed the tissue back in her pocket, took hold of her cart, and as she began to walk, she stood straighter. Once again, the spring was back in her step.

It was starting to get dark, and rain began to fall. The two watchers turned to return home, but as they did so, they could hear the woman calling, hoping she wasn't calling to them. They turned and saw she was calling out to someone far into the woods. A dog ran out to greet her.

She opened her arms and picked up the little creature, holding it tightly speaking gently, rubbing its back. The dog licked her face and wagged its tail. After a few moments, she put the dog down, and both walked into the woods together letting the rain wash away all their sorrows with the hopes that tomorrow would be a better day.

Despite the weather, the watchers cautiously followed her further into the woods until they saw her enter a worn-down hunter's cabin barely large enough to accommodate the woman and her small companion. They tried to move forward to get a better look when they heard the dog barking. The woman came to the broken doorway, looked around, and saw the watchers.

The welcoming smile on her face was that of an angel welcoming souls into heaven.

"How wonderful to see my friends! Did you enjoy the tomatoes? Come in, please, join us for a bite to eat. But you must hurry, pretty soon it will be too dark, and you won't be able to see yourselves home." It was impossible for them to refuse. After all, they were caught spying on the poor woman.

They entered the dark interior and noticed how surprisingly clean it was. All her found treasures were spread throughout the area, and a clean, old cloth covered the small table in the center of the cabin.

"I seldom get visitors. It's a pleasure to see you again."

"Do you live here all alone?" asked the older watcher.

"I used to live in a home on Norton Street. My son used to take care of me, but he died a year ago, and I'm afraid my daughter-in-law had little patience with an old woman like me." As she spoke, it seemed that her speech was more easily understood, and her calmness put the watchers at ease. "When she went on a cruise last year, she locked me out. I doubt she even knows I'm gone or even cares. I remembered seeing this place on one of my walks years ago. My son and I used to come here and just talk. It was our place to remember the good times. So, here I am, a forgotten soul with no place else to go."

When she was finished talking, the watchers looked at one another and almost in unison asked, "Would you like to join us for Thanksgiving dinner? Our whole family will be here. We'd love to have you."

She still walks around the block every day pushing her cart. The little dog walks along side of her, and now she always has a place to stop to have a cup of tea. Although she still prefers to live in the little cabin with the memories of her son, she always has a place in the watcher's home. She is no longer the forgotten soul; just temporarily misplaced.

31

THE HURRICANE

It was unusually cold that day with a mist and breeze causing the leaves in the trees to rustle, making an eerie sound. Adam was leaning against a tree, sleeping lightly, not wanting anyone to take his few belongings. His clothes were damp and dirty with the smell of spilled whisky. If one looked closely, you could tell he was younger than he looked, with a month's growth of beard on his dirt-smudged face. He wasn't bad looking, but the look of despair and heartache showed in his features.

The wind picked up speed, blowing wet leaves and debris onto his face. He woke and looked around. Usually by now, there would be people hustling off to work, walking their dogs or jogging on the several paths throughout the park; but now, it was empty.

He got up slowly. His back was stiff. He gathered his few possessions and headed towards the alley where garbage from the night before had been placed. He was usually able to find enough food there for his breakfast and lunch. Dinner, he would worry about later.

On his way, he noticed an intense quiet. Stores were closed; not much traffic. As he looked towards the town square, he saw a man trying to carry several bags of groceries with not much success. He walked over to him and asked, "What's going on? Where is everyone?"

The man looked up, annoyed, trying to balance his bags.

"Haven't you heard there's a hurricane coming? It should be here within a few hours. It's moving faster than expected. Go crawl back into the hole you came from and leave me alone."

With that, one of his bags fell to the street spilling out a dozen or so oranges, bread, and a container of milk. Adam knelt down to help pick up the articles for the man, slipping one of the oranges into his pocket.

"I don't need your help you, lousy SOB. Go steal from someone else. Put that orange back, and get out of my way!" With that, he hit him with his umbrella, picked up the remaining few pieces from the ground, and walked away leaving Adam on the sidewalk sitting in a puddle of milk.

At that moment, a gust of wind blew his hat off, sending it down the street. The clouds were dark in various shades of grey, moving quickly across the sky. He looked towards the park. The trees were almost bent over due to the force of the wind. He lived on the street for years and was used to finding shelter. He better start now before all the other homeless took his spots. It was starting to rain.

He rushed over to the homeless shelter, but he doubted there would be room for him. He survived hurricane Camelle in 1969 with a land speed of 190 mph. But he had a home then. A safe place to stay. Now, he had nowhere to go.

By the time he reached the shelter, it was full, and he knew the school shelter in district 63 on Elm Street would be full as well since that was always the first to be filled because they had beds and always a hot meal. The old, abandoned church south of town had a basement, easily accessible. He would go there. He could hear the wind building up in speed, and he could already see some of its destruction. Trees were down, and wires were bouncing off the ground. He reached the church and climbed through the cellar window.

He was not alone.

In the corner, huddled, shaking, was the man he saw earlier. The one with the groceries. They looked at one another. He nodded, but the man remained silent.

"I guess we meet again. We'll have to make the best of it until the weather clears. My name is Adam."

The man turned away huddling closer to the corner.

In that instant, they heard a LOUD bang overhead. The ceiling cracked.

"We're going to die!" the man yelled, almost in tears.

"No, we'll be alright. I've been through worse and survived with no more than a scratch. I'm not going to ask how you managed to find yourself here, so how about opening up your bags, and we have a bite to eat? Things always seem brighter when you have a little food in your stomach."

Reluctantly, the man opened up one of his bags and handed him an orange and slice of bread. They both ate until another sound broke their silence. The wind was picking up speed and broke one of the cellar windows, allowing the cold, wind and rain into their area of refuge.

"Come on sir, let me help you up. We have to move away from the windows or else we'll be drenched as well as being in danger of broken glass."

The man held out his hand. Adam helped him up, and together, they picked up the bags and moved to the other side of the basement. Another crash. There, where they had been sitting, was a tree trunk that actually sailed through the window, embedding itself into the wall.

"You saved my life."

"Everyone's life is worth saving."

More items from the church crashed through the ceiling. Adam placed a few discarded church pews against the wall, allowing them to lie down above the foot of water that had accumulated on the floor. Hours passed. The man handed him a bottle of water and a Baby Ruth candy bar. For the first time, Adam saw the man smile.

In time, the wind died down, and they fell asleep.

When they awoke, only a slight breeze was present. They crawled out the window into the sun.

Looking around, all they could see was water and broken trees with debris everywhere. Buildings were down, people were crying, and fires could be seen in the distance.

"I'm going home. I can't stand all this. What are you going to do?"

"I have no home to go to. This," Adam said extending his arm and passing it around indicating the mass destruction, "is my home. I guess I had better start cleaning it up."

He walked over to a shopkeeper and helped him repair the door to his store, then he handed a little girl her doll that had floated down the road by his feet. He then continued down the street, helping where he could. He looked back at the man he had spent the night with, whose life he saved, and waved for him to join him, but the man simply turned and walked away as if the previous night had never happened.

32
THE WEDDING

She seemed to fly out of bed quickly, putting on her warm slippers and fuzzy robe. Today was a very special day. She rushed into the bathroom and splashed some cool water on her face and brushed her teeth. Down the stairs she went, making a quick turn to the left as she reached the floor and entered the kitchen. She took two eggs, butter, and a carton of orange juice from the fridge and placed them on the counter as she reached up to get the bread. The frying pan was still on the stove from last night's dinner. She placed one scoop of butter in the pan and cracked open both eggs with one hand, letting them fall to the pan. One quick swish with the whisk, and they were left on low heat while she placed the bread in the toaster. While she waited for the toast and eggs to be finished, she poured herself a glass of juice, sat down, and looked out the window.

It was a familiar sight. The view was the same now as it had been all her life. She loved what she saw. She would miss it, but it was time to move on. She could have gone to college and married, but other commitments blocked her way, and her own life was put on hold. But today was different. She was doing something for herself; something she had been waiting for her whole life.

Toast popped, eggs cooked, her last breakfast in this old house. Yes, she would miss it, but it was time.

Up the stairs she dashed. She laid out her clothes then went back into the bathroom to shower and dry her hair. She even put on some cologne given to her by her mother when she was in high school. How many times had she taken the time to put on cologne? Not many. The bottle was almost full. She placed some makeup on her face and looked at herself in the mirror.

Not bad, she thought as she smiled at her reflection. *Not bad at all.*

She then walked into the bedroom, made her bed for the last time, then slowly opened the window overlooking the corn field and mountains in the distance. She could smell the lilacs just coming into full bloom and the scent of newly cut hay. She took a deep breath, wanting this moment to be engrained in her memory forever.

She started to dress, carefully putting on the petticoat and dress her mother had worn years ago. It was slightly discolored from years of storage in the attic with a small stain along the bottom, probably from trailing along the ground as her mother walked. It fit her perfectly except for the length since it no longer touched the ground but flowed gently as she went from place to place getting ready. Finally, she was finished dressing and looked at herself, again, in the mirror. She pinned a few wild flowers in her soft, curly hair.

One last thing needed to be added before she left, she went to her jewelry box and opened it, seeing the familiar ballerina twirl around. The music had long-since stopped playing, but the tune would never be forgotten. From the box, she took a small, heart-shaped pendant with a thin, gold chain that held two pictures, one of her mother and one of her father. As she looked at the pictures, long-since faded, a tear rolled down her cheek.

"My day has finally come," she said, "I regret nothing, but it is now time to move on." She placed the locket around her neck, took one last quick look at herself, smiled, and quietly went down the stairs and out the front door.

Today was her day; her wedding day. No more responsibilities; no more waiting. It took her many years to find someone to love, but when she did, she knew it right away. It took him a little longer to realize the attraction, but when he did, he proposed, and they set the date for one month. Why wait? Time was short.

The little neighborhood church was the same one her parents were married in many years ago. Only this time, the couple walking down the aisle will be a little different. The groom is 87 years of age, and the bride is 84.

33

THE USUAL SUSPECTS

Chapter One

Captain Monroe walked into the station with his usual bouncy, quick step, taking his coat off as he walked and hanging it on the rack. He looked over at the new rooky, Officer Clifton James.

"We got a dead one on the marina of 5th and Queen. Take a squad car and round up the usual suspects."

"Hey," said James, "ain't that a line from Casablanca?"

"Yeah, the greatest movie ever made. I loved that movie."

"But boss, there are no suspects. The guy is just dead."

"If you learn anything working with me kid, you'll learn that no one is 'just dead.'"

Cliff shook his head and put on his jacket.

"I'm right on it, boss."

"Don't call me 'boss.' Until you earn your dues, call me 'captain.'"

"Sure, boss, sure."

Monroe just shrugged. He'd make a good detective out of the boy if it was the last thing he did. James was right about one thing. There WERE no suspects. And there were no CSI units in this small town. If this case was going to be solved, it would be with lots of old-fashioned deduction and hard work.

The only reason Monroe asked for another officer was because he knew he was going to retire soon. His previous assistant detective, a quiet but competent officer, recently died in an unexplained accident while fishing. It was a sorry loss for everyone, including his fiancée, Nicole, of only two weeks.

After several hours, James returned to the station.

"Well, what did you get?" Monroe asked.

"Not much boss. The deceased, a Mr. Edmond Kramer, has a houseboat on the *Southside Pier*. It's a bit small, but big enough. The pier is kind of out of the way, not in a built-up area with limited access to it. Private, snobby district, if you know what I mean. I checked it out. Had to get the pier supervisor to let me in. Not very cooperative. Check him out later.

"Anyway, I went down to the dock and looked for the boat. It's the last one on pier #3, slip #9. You know what, boss? The boat wasn't even locked. I just walked right in. Cute little boat. Curtains, nice rug, little table set for two…"

"Get on with it, what did you find that would help us crack this case?"

James gave him a look of dejection but continued, "Like I said, the table was set for two. There was a can of coffee on the counter, but no sign of any percolator. Napkins, candles, and a little bouquet of flowers, they were starting to wilt, so I gave them a little water."

"Don't get off the subject kid!" Monroe was getting a little impatient.

"There was no food anyplace. Every plate and glass was clean as a whistle. The only thing that seemed off kilter was that considering how clean everything was, there were some rodent droppings and one black, man's deck shoe under the table. I called the coroner to see if our vic had only one shoe. Said he'd check after he did the prelims and get back to me."

"That's it, that's all you got?

"No, actually, there is something else. Did you know your ex-partner had a boat on that very same pier?"

Chapter Two

Captain Monroe knew Pete had a boat he used for local fishing. He certainly didn't think he had a big enough boat to be docked at such an exclusive place like the Southside Pier. There may be more about Detective Peter O'Rourke that he didn't know. He decided to check out the houseboat for himself. Not that he felt his rookie didn't do a good job, but he didn't believe in coincidences!

Monroe encountered the same, uncooperative superintendent, but since Monroe looked and acted nothing like a rookie, he obtained quick access to the pier. He also found out where O'Rourke had his boat. It was now owned by someone else and was only two slips from the deceased, Edmond Kramer.

"Who owns that slip now?" he asked the superintendent.

"Oh, I forget her name, but she's a pretty little thing."

"Was she around any time over the last two days?"

"I didn't see her, but I can check the in/out log. But not everyone fills it out. It's mainly for the inexperienced boaters, so they feel a more secure when they leave the marina."

"Where were you last night Mr...."

"Mr. Woodruff. Am I a suspect in something?"

"Not yet. The owner of that houseboat was found dead this morning. I think he was killed right here in front of your nose."

"I didn't do any killing, and I certainly wouldn't do anything so stupid as kill someone where I work."

"No one said you were stupid. But I do think you should answer my question. Where were you last night, Mr. Woodruff?"

"I was down at the Jumping Frog having a few beers and dancing the two-step with some of the waitresses. You can check it out."

"Don't worry, I will."

Chapter Three

For the next two days, nothing seemed to pan out. Mr. Woodruff's alibi was confirmed, and further search of the houseboat turned up nothing. The mysterious woman never signed the log book, and it seemed only about three people signed it, and they were, as the supervisor said, all rookies when it came to boating. The only surprise was the coroner's report. Seems our friend Mr. Kramer was poisoned.

Monroe was feeling a bit anxious. Nothing seemed to be fitting together. Prints taken were of the deceased and those of the new owner of O'Rourke's boat, Nicole Freeman, a con artist with a record of running scams in south Florida. She apparently served time and let out on good behavior.

"Come on, kid, let's see if we can find our *Lady of the Lake* and see what she can tell us."

Both Monroe and James took another trip to the marina. This time, the superintendent was more than helpful and let them right in. When they arrived at the boat, there was a woman sitting on deck, smoking, having a drink. She looked up and with only a slight look of surprise said, "Why, Detective Monroe, long time no see."

No one could have been more surprised than Monroe. This Nicole Freeman was the same "Nicky" he knew as the fiancée of his partner and friend, Pete O'Rourke. Whatever was going on here was certainly starting to smell fishy.

"Nicky, good to see you. I thought you moved back south after Pete's death." Monroe was curious as to how she ended up with Pete's boat. Somehow, the sweet "Nicky" he knew was not the same hardcore Nicky he saw before him.

"No, when I found out that Pete left me the boat, I moved in. Is there something I can do for you?"

James noted the suspicious look on Monroe's face and answered, "Yes, as a matter of fact there is, Ms. Freeman, we'd like to look around if you don't mind."

"I don't mind you looking around, but what is the reason you are interested in my boat?"

"A man was murdered just down the dock here. We're just doing a routine check, looking for the usual suspects, you know how it is. Not saying you're a suspect or anything…"

Without waiting for permission, the two men went on board and started searching. It didn't take long before James found a black, man's deck shoe under some old anchor chains on the aft deck. He joined Monroe down below to tell him of his discovery when Monroe pointed out some plants growing in the bathroom.

"Looks like our Ms. Freeman has been growing some recreational weed."

"No, boss, that's not marijuana. It's a castor bean plant; comes from Brazil. It's one of the most poisonous naturally occurring substances known—Resin. Easy to make. You can get the directions from the internet."

"I don't want to know how you come to know all this stuff. You're becoming more useful than I gave you credit for. Looks like we actually have a suspect. It's about time."

As they were leaving officer James noticed something else—rat droppings leading to the downstairs cabin.

"Ms. Freeman," he asked, "have you been having trouble with rodents aboard ship?"

Nicole looked straight into his eyes, her expression cold, and answered, "Why, yes. As a matter of fact, everyone on this side of the marina has been having trouble. I tried traps, but they didn't work. The rats are much too large for them. I tried other methods and still haven't gotten rid of them."

A smile crossed Monroe's face.

"What other methods have you tried?"

"Why Detective Monroe, don't play games with me. You already know the answer. I tried poison."

Chapter Four

After they got back to the office, a call was made to the coroner, and sure enough, there was a shoe missing from the body, and the shoe they found in Nicole's boat was an exact match. Tox screening showed traces of Resin in the vic's system. The more things started to add up the more Monroe admired his new assistant.

James rushed into the office carrying a file folder and handed it to Monroe.

"Look at this, boss. You'll never guess..."

"Just tell me. I don't have time for games."

"Well, seems that our vic and our Ms. Freeman share a rather colorful past. Several of the scams she pulled involved an accomplice. Guess who? I know, I know, no games. Mr. Edmond Kramer was arrested along with her on three occasions. They were rather CLOSE friends, if you know what I mean. But since her release from jail, there is no record of them being together."

"Good work, kid. Now all we have to do is find out if they were up to something and if that something involved my ex-partner, Pete. Let's see if our 'friendly' superintendent ever saw them together. Another thing, recheck the dock and see if we missed anything. Make it quick."

It didn't take James long to return with some news.

"The superintendent was very cooperative. I didn't tell him he was no longer a suspect; thought he would be more forthcoming if I didn't. I asked him if there was a problem with rats, and he said no. So I figure Kramer must have been in her boat at one time or another to get rat droppings on his shoes then under his table. The super said he saw the vic with Nicole once at the Jumping Frog. At first, he didn't pay any attention, but he did take notice when they started to argue. Kramer grabbed her arm at one point, but another customer stepped in and told him to leave. He's not sure, but he thinks she left with the guy. I checked with the bartender, and he remembers Nicole. Said she was hot. After the fight, he remembers her telling the guy about a problem with rats on a friend's boat. The guy said he had just the thing. He went outside and brought back a coffee can with a plant in it and gave it to her. After that, they left, and he didn't see them come in again."

"That's the best news I've heard all day. Get down to Kramer's boat and bring me back that coffee can. I think there's more in that can than just coffee."

As James was leaving Kramer's boat with a can of coffee, he noticed that Nicole's boat was not in its slip. He hurried to the superintendent's office only to find him dead behind the desk with a hole in his forehead. He called the Coast Guard and then called Monroe as he headed to his car to bring the coffee can for prints and verification of its contents. It was now time to round up the usual suspects.

Thanks to the Coast Guard, Nicole was picked up with the guy from the bar. Good thing, since she intended to do the same to him as she did to O'Rourke, Kramer, and the superintendent. She didn't want any witnesses left behind.

Chapter Five

Monroe took the file and placed it in the "closed" box.

"Well kid, you did a fine job on this one." Monroe looked at his new partner with admiration. "I always knew Pete was a little naïve, but I really thought he found a match when he found Nicky. She seemed to genuinely love the guy. She was just using him as a cover for another one of her scams."

James turned in his chair and added, "When Pete found out about her past and connection with Kramer, she recruited Kramer to kill him then she killed Kramer with the Resin. I suppose when we started nosing around, she knew she had to get rid of the guy from the bar and the superintendent."

Again, Monroe seemed pleased with James.

"So what you are saying is she remembered seeing him at the Jumping Frog and didn't want him giving any more information about her to the police."

"That's about it, boss."

This time, Monroe didn't mind the kid calling him boss. He just turned to James and said, "That about raps it up, *Officer* James, keep up the good work."

34
YOU NEVER KNOW WHAT
YOU MIGHT FIND

Jane sat at the table drinking her first cup of morning coffee, reading the paper.

"Look here, Pete. It says here that a woman, age 87, is being released from prison today. She has terminal cancer. She's been incarcerated for 50 years, and all that time she's maintained her innocence. She was found guilty of killing her husband of 19 years. Her case was appealed twice. No gun or bullet was ever found."

Pete looked up from reading the sports section.

"How could there be no bullet?"

"Seems the bullet went right through the poor guy, and it was several days before the body was found, giving her plenty of time to hide the gun."

"Jane, it's too early to be playing detective. You're no longer working in the DA's office. Did you check the paper for any yard sales or flea markets today? I'm still trying to find a small plug in fridge for the car for when we do our cross-country yard sales."

"I don't know why you just don't buy one. How expensive can they be?"

"You know I enjoy the 'hunt,' and besides, I hate to pay retail."

Jane handed Pete the "Yard Sale" section.

"Here, I'm going over to the shop. Toni called, and she found a clock I might be interested in. See you later."

She kissed Pete goodbye and off she went. When she entered the Antique and Heirloom Shop, she immediately smiled as she breathed in the musty smell with the anticipation of finding something special. She collected old clocks and photos. She never understood how someone could throw photos away. When someone snapped a picture, it was usually commemorating a happy event. A photo kept the memory alive, but as generations passed and no one was left to keep that memory, the photo was discarded and, at times, ending up in places like here.

Toni greeted Jane as she walked into the storage room.

"Hello there. Someone brought in a box with old papers and photos. There's also a clock. I'm afraid it's beyond repair as far as getting it to work, but I think you'll be able to fix it making a nice show piece out of it. It's over there in the corner."

With that, Toni was out the door to wait on a customer.

Jane was so excited when she saw the weather-worn box. She pulled up a chair, sat down and lifted the box onto her lap. Yes, the clock, an 1890 Black Forest, Cuckoo, Buck, was broken. It had a small, round hole in the front with something lodged in the back of it. She placed it back into the box, knowing she could fix it without much trouble.

As her fingers flipped through the old photos and letters, they touched a book lying on the bottom of the box. She picked it up. It appeared to be a diary. The flimsy lock was easily opened, and the pages were marred, dried, and wrinkled, as if they had been set in dampness for many, many years. The writing was somewhat faded and, in parts, completely washed away. The dates on the opening pages set back over sixty years.

When she got home, Pete was standing at the kitchen sink, cleaning his find from the yard sale.

"Well, I see you got your refrigerator. How much did that cost ya?"

"Only five bucks. Can you believe it? I already tried it out. Works like a charm. What did you get? "

"Just an old box with some junk." Pete saw her smile and knew she found more than junk.

In her office, she laid the papers on the shelf, then put the diary on the acetone free mat. Jane turned a brittle page with her tweezers and read what she could of the first legible entry:

1942: ...he is such a wonderful man. I can't believe my luck. He's a soldier home on leave. He says he loves me, but I'm sure that isn't true for...only a short time. If only...

1944: Things seem to be moving so fast. Am I doing the right thing? I love him, but can I be sure he... strange feelings and moods. Soon we will be married.

1951: He said that if I have this child, he'll leave me. Perhaps that would be for the best. I don't know...his verbal abuse for much longer. I thought our child would change things. Make things...It's not too late to abort the pregnancy. Would it be fair to bring a child into this world when I'm not sure what the future might hold? He told me it wasn't his child. That I was drunk. I don't remember drinking...if only I could remember...

She heard Pete call her from the kitchen.

"Jane come on down, see how great my fridge looks now that it's all cleaned up. Let's go out to dinner to celebrate our good day."

"Be right down!" Jane put her things away and walked over and looked into the hole of the clock. Whatever was inside was hard to see. *I'll have to check that out later,* she thought. Pete was right. It was a good day; time to celebrate! She hadn't eaten since breakfast.

The next day was cloudy, a good day to stay indoors. Pete had gone to work, and she was about to have her second cup of coffee when the phone rang. She looked at the caller ID. It was the *Citizen's Press,* a small local newspaper that hired her to do interviews when no one else wanted the assignment. She let the answering machine take the message. She took her coffee and went up to her office to repair the clock, and she had just about every tool imaginable to do the job. She carefully laid the clock on the workbench, positioned the light directly into the hole, and put on her magnifying glasses. The hidden object was small, round and silver with quite a bit of corrosion. She got up to get her extraction tool when she noticed the diary sitting on her desk. She was sure she had put it away last night, but there it was, open to the next entry. The writing, although much clearer, was written in a more delicate hand.

> *1960: How many more times can I go to the emergency room before they become suspicious? How many more broken bones can I sustain? How long can I keep covering up my bruises?*
>
> *My heart is saddened by what I have become. My mind is…I've become vicious and want revenge, and one day, I will have it.*
>
> *1961: I hear the child cry. No, the child was never born, yet I hear her. I pretend she is here with me as I am locked in the closet, which has now become my home. He lets me out only when the stench becomes too unbearable. Then I bathe and bathe the child I know does not exist, only in my sick mind.*

*1962: I have a plan…it will work. I must wait until
he lets me out again.*

The phone rings again, but this time Jane picked it up.

"Where have you been? I've been trying to reach you. I have an assignment for you, right up your alley. I think your experience in the DA's office makes you perfect for this job. Come on down to the office, and we'll go over the details."

John Fleming was a detective for the Los Angeles Police Department, retired for 20 years. He now spent most of his time fishing but did detective work on the side. He had an unusual case that he felt Jane could help him with, so after the usual pleasantries, he got right to the point.

"Jane, I want you to interview, more precisely, I want you to question a Mrs. Anna Henderson."

"And just who is this Ms. Henderson?"

"Surely you've read about her in the paper. She was just released from prison after 50 years."

"Yes, I read about her in the paper, but why should I or anyone else want to interview her?"

John sat back and put his legs up on his desk.

"Because I think she's innocent."

Jane's head was spinning by the time she returned home. Ms. Henderson, Anna, was not at all what she expected. She may be 87, dying of cancer, but she was strong. When she asked her point blank if she killed her husband she said, "NO!" then looked away and added, "I killed someone else." They talked for almost three hours before her condition prohibited her from continuing. Her body weakened, and her thoughts drifted from past to present. Jane arranged for another meeting just as Anna drifted into sleep.

That night, Jane spent most of the evening cleaning the clock. She finally retrieved what appeared to be a .38 caliber bullet from the hole and placed it in an evidence bag. She then started to go through the pictures and letters that were in the weathered box she had gotten from the antique store. The letters were to a serviceman dated back to 1942 but were so damaged that trying to read them was futile. There were several pictures showing a man and smiling woman, apparently on their wedding day; another with them holding a "sold" sign standing on the steps of a small colonial house. The third was that of a very happy, pregnant woman sitting next to a not-so-happy man. She placed the pictures back in the box except for a wedding photo, which she placed in another evidence bag, placing both bags in her briefcase, intending to show them to John in the morning. Jane then took a seat by the window to finish reading the diary. The handwriting had been changing from ascending to the right meaning optimistic, having faith in the future, feelings of love, excited, and joyous, to having a descending slant showing pessimism, fatigue, discouragement, depression, and illness.

> *1963: It's almost time. This time, when he hit me, it took a long time before I could stop the bleeding. I feel weak. I found a loaded gun hidden in the closet I've spent so much time in. Perhaps he hoped I would take my own life, but I'll surprise him tomorrow when I take his instead. God forgive me.*

The next day, Jane took the evidence bag with the bullet and gave it to John.

"Let me know if this matches what made the hole that killed Mr. Henderson."

"Where'd you get that?"

"Tell you later."

Then she went to meet with Anna. Anna was sitting up, waiting for Jane. She was anxious to tell her side of the story.

Jane said nothing as she took the photo from her bag and handed it to Anna. With frail, feeble, fingers Anna took the photo and placed it on her lap. Tears fell from her saddened face.

"It seems just like yesterday. I was so in love that I never would have thought our lives would have ended the way it did."

Jane then handed the diary over to its author. Anna's both hands shook as she held her precious friend of so many years ago.

"This was my only companion. The only one I could talk to. Everyone thought so fondly of my husband; who would believe me if I told them how cruelly he treated me? Every day it was another bruise, another harsh word, another broken bone. I could have taken all of that until the baby. He killed my unborn child, so eventually, I had to kill him. He was no longer the man I married. He became someone else; someone I didn't even know. It was worth 50 years in prison to know that he could not hurt anyone again. Do you think there is a place for me in hell?"

Jane never got a chance to answer her question because it was just then that Anna closed her eyes and felt the pain for the last time.

The bullet was from a small frame .357 Smith and Wesson Magnum that had been registered to a neighbor of Mr. Henderson, who had reported it stolen. It was never found. When Anna was originally apprehended, she was found in an old loft just outside downtown LA. Now that the area was being cleaned up, the old lofts were being torn down and cleaned out. That's how the old box ended up being sent to the antique shop.

But for Jane, she fixed the clock and has it hanging in her dining room alongside the photo of a very brave and beautiful bride.

35
THINGS ARE NOT ALWAYS WHAT THEY SEEM

She laid huddled in the dark corner on her make shift bed of old towels and newspapers. Her meal of dried food and warm water only partially filled her belly. It was a long time since she had a good meal provided by her mother, long since gone. She must have been in a basement, for it was damp, although clean, with the smell of mold.

At the end of the hall was "the man" sitting at an old, worn wooden desk piled high with papers drinking a cup of stale coffee, reading a week-old paper that would soon be part of her bed. He never treated her badly but didn't treat her well either. Occasionally, he would smile, giving her a look that only showed sadness and despair.

The phone rang. She lifted her head, startled by the loud ring in an otherwise quiet space. He picked it up and spoke quietly to whoever was on the other end. She heard others, and she was grateful that she was not alone. He slammed the phone down, picked up a set of keys, and headed down the long corridor. A tear fell from his eye, down his cheek, and onto his soiled, dark blue shirt. His heavy boots made a pounding sound so heavy, it made her make-shift bed shake. Her body shook as well.

After selecting a key, she could hear him open one of the doors just beyond her vision. There was a commotion. There was a heart wrenching cry, then silence.

She partially stuck her head through a hole, the same hole that was used to pass through her food. She could see others that were much older, thin, with a sad, forgotten look. Yet there were younger ones too, playing, jumping up and down. The man didn't seem to notice them.

The next morning, she could see the sun shining through the dingy window above "the man's" cluttered desk. He was putting food in bowls…so many. He seemed to be in a better mood today.

Again, the phone rang. He picked it up. This time, he seemed happy, making animated gestures with his hand. He grabbed another key from the wall and headed towards her room. He stopped whistling as he placed the key in the lock and opened the door.

"Come on out, girl, this is your lucky day."

She remained still, hunkering down in the corner, expecting to be whipped although she never had been since she arrived. He entered the room and bent down to pick her up. As her body quivered, she looked into his eyes. There was kindness there, somewhere.

He brought her over to the desk and placed her on a pile of papers.

"It's a good thing for you that you're so cute; otherwise, you might have stayed here awhile." He bent down and tilted her chin. She gave a little cry. He smiled.

The main door opened, and another man with a kind face walked through.

"The man" handed the other man a pen.

"Sign here," he said, "and she's all yours."

He took the pen and signed the papers, then looked at her, smiled, and reached down and picked her up and held her to his chest.

"Let's get out of here, little one, and let's go home."

Her little tail wagged as she licked his face. The word home never sounded so good.